PREDESTINED

by Abbi Glines

D1527036

Predestined
Copyright © 2012 by Abbi Glines

This book is a work of fiction and any resemblance to any person, living or dead, any place, events or occurrences, is purely coincidental. The characters and story lines are created from the author's imagination or are used fictitiously.

Editor: Stephanie T. Lott a.k.a. Bibliophile

Cover illustration by Stephanie Mooney © 2012 For information on the cover art, please contact mooneydesigns@gmail.com

Abbi Glines
16125 County Road 13
Fairhope, AL 36532
Printed in The United States of America

Dedication

To my daughter, Annabelle. You have an "old soul" my sweet girl. The wisdom of your choices and the kindness in your actions never cease to amaze me. I'm so incredibly proud of you.

The narrow damp street was uninhabited. Jazz music could be heard from a distance but the sound was faint. The further I walked away from the scattered street lights and into the darkness the more the sounds of laughter, street cars and the traditional vibrant music only found in the Big Easy melted away. I'd been here before, countless times. Death was often met on these dark streets. But tonight, I wasn't here to take a soul. I was here for other reasons. Reasons I was just now piecing together. The fury raging inside me was hard to control. I'd been reckless. Me! A freaking almighty Deity, let something dangerous slip right past my radar completely undetected. How could I have let this happen? I knew the answer. Pagan. She consumed me. My thoughts. My desires. My purpose. I'd been unable to see anything with the glow of Pagan blinding me from everything else. Now, I had to find out why and then I had to fix this. Because Pagan Moore was mine. Her life, her soul, her heart it was all mine. Nothing was going to stand in my way. No ancient curse. No soulless boy. And absolutely *no* Voodoo spirit lord.

CHAPTER ONE

Pagan

I'd just turned around to watch the pretty balloons. I liked the pink one best. It reminded me of bubblegum. I'd been trying to think of something I could promise Mommy I'd do if she'd buy me one. Maybe clean out from under my bed or maybe straighten the shoes in her closet. But it had only been a second that I'd stopped and thought about it. Now, my mommy was gone. Tears clouded my vision and I let out a panicked sob. She'd warned me I could get lost in the crowd if I didn't keep up. Normally I held her hand when we were in crowds but today she was carrying an armload of her books. It had been my responsibility not to lose her. But I had. Where would I sleep? I glanced nervously around at the people covering the busy streets. The Arts and Entertainment Festival had brought people from all over to our small town. Reaching up to wipe my eyes so I could find a police officer to help me, I sniffled and for a second forgot my crisis when the smell of funnel cake reached me.

"Don't cry, I'll help you."

Frowning, I studied the boy in front of me. His blond hair was cut short and his big friendly eyes looked concerned. I had never seen him before. He didn't go to my school. Maybe he was a tourist. Whoever he was, I knew he couldn't help me. He was just a kid too.

"I lost my mommy," I muttered, feeling embarrassed that he'd caught me crying.

He nodded then held out his hand. "I know. I'm going to take you back to her. It's okay, I promise."

Swallowing the lump in my throat, I thought about his offer. Could he help me? Two sets of eyes looking for a police officer were better than one, I guess. "Um, if you could just help me look for a police officer so he could find her that would be nice."

He smiled at me like he thought I was funny. I hadn't been joking and nothing about this was cause to smile.

"I really know where she is. Trust me," his hand was still outstretched toward me.

Frowning, I thought about all the reasons this was probably a bad idea. He couldn't be much older than me. Maybe he was like seven at the most. But he seemed so sure of himself. Besides, he wasn't an adult stranger. He wouldn't kidnap me.

"Okay," I finally replied, slipping my hand in his. His face appeared to relax. I sure hoped he didn't get us both lost.

"Where are your parents?" I asked, suddenly realizing maybe they could help.

"Around here somewhere," he replied and a small frown touched his forehead. "Come with me," his voice was gentle but firm. He kind of reminded me of an adult.

I kept up with him as he wove a path through the bodies in our way. I tried to glance up at people *as we hurried by to see if I recognized anyone but I wasn't having any luck.*

"There she is," the boy said as he stopped our pursuit and pointed a finger toward the sidewalk up ahead.

Sure enough, there was my mommy and she was really upset. A scared look was on her face as she grabbed the arms of people passing by and spoke frantically to them. I realized she was looking for me. Needing to reassure her I pulled my hand from the boy's and took off running in her direction.

Her big, round, terrified eyes found me and she let out a sob then began to call my name, "Pagan, Pagan, Pagan!"

My eyes opened and the ceiling fan greeted me, the sun streamed in through my window and my frustrated mother banged on my door.

"You're going to be late for school. Now get up right this minute"

"I'm awake. Calm down," I called out in a voice hoarse from sleep and forced myself to sit up.

"Finally, I swear girl, you're getting harder and harder to wake up. Now hurry up. I've made pancakes for breakfast."

"Okay, okay," I muttered and rubbed my sleepy eyes. I'd had another one of those dreams. Why was I dreaming about snippets from my childhood and why was I just now realizing that the same boy helped me out in each of my traumatic experiences? I had forgotten about that day at the festival, getting lost. But it had happened. I remembered it now. And that boy... he'd been there. Why was he so familiar?

My bedroom door opened softly and my concerns vanished at the sight of Dank stepping inside my room. He'd started using my door instead of just appearing out of nowhere and scaring the bejesus out of me. It was a small request that he always tried to honor.

"She's making pancakes... do you think she'd let me have a few when I show up to pick you up for school?"

His voice was deep and hypnotic. Even now, I wanted to sigh and bask in the warmth it sent through me. I stood up and closed the short distance between us. Stopping right in front of him I placed both hands on his chest and smiled up into his startling blue eyes.

"Until Leif shows up you're not exactly her favorite person. You know that."

He frowned and I hated that my mother was being so difficult. I didn't like making him frown. But unfortunately with my exboyfriend suddenly missing my mother was blaming it on me breaking up with him for another guy. It isn't like I can tell her the truth. She'd think I was insane for real this time and I'd never be let out of the mental house.

"Hey," Dank said reaching out a hand to cup my face, "stop it. This isn't your fault. Besides we both know I don't need food. Her pancakes just smell incredible."

It can come in handy when he read my emotions. Then other times it annoys me to no end.

"Well, maybe if you would explain to me what exactly you meant by 'Leif isn't human' then I wouldn't feel so guilty."

Dank sighed and sank down on my bed pulling me onto his lap. His blue eyes still held a trace of the glow that ignited in them when he took a soul at the body's time of death. I wrapped my arms around his neck trying very hard to keep the serious expression on my face. When he was this close it was hard to think coherently.

"I told you that I'm not completely positive what Leif is exactly. All I know is he has no soul. That's the only thing I know for certain."

I tucked a lock of his dark hair behind his ear and decided to give pouting a try.

"Well, what do you *think* he is?"

Dank raised his eyebrows and a sexy dimple producing grin appeared on his face. "Pouting, Pagan? Really? I expected more from you than that. When did my girl go all underhanded on me...hmmm?"

I shoved his chest and stuck out my tongue, "That isn't underhanded."

His amused laugh sent shivers of pleasure down my spine. "Yes, Pagan it is. I don't like for you to pout. You know that."

"PAGAN, GET DOWN HERE AND EAT! YOU'RE GOING TO BE LATE," my mother's voice loudly carried up the stairs.

"Go eat. I'll be outside in twenty minutes to pick you up," he whispered in my ear before kissing my temple and standing me up. I put my hands on my hips to argue but he vanished before I could get a word out.

"Just because you're Death doesn't mean you can get away with being rude," I hissed into the empty room just in case he was close enough to hear me.

With an annoyed humph, I headed to the bathroom to get ready.

"You're not going to have time to sit down and eat breakfast if you intend on making it to first period before the bell," my mother said frowning as I walked into the kitchen.

"I know, I'll just take a pancake with me," I reached for one of the pancakes she'd piled on the plate in the center of the table and felt instantly guilty for taking so long to get ready. She'd obviously went out of her way to make a nice hot meal for me to start my day and all I had time for was to grab a pancake and eat it on my way out to Dank's Jeep.

"I'm sorry, Mom. I overslept. Thank you for this," I said leaning in to kiss her cheek before picking up my book bag off the kitchen table.

"I need to get you an alarm clock," she mumbled and pulled out a chair to sit down.

"I promise tomorrow I'll get up thirty minutes earlier. Put the left overs in the fridge and we'll heat them up in the microwave in the morning and enjoy them together."

She didn't smile but instead frowned into her coffee cup. Dangit, she knew how to make me feel bad.

Pulling out a chair, I sat down knowing I'd be jumping right back up in less than three minutes but I wanted to make her happy and I wanted to ask her about my dream.

"Do you remember when I was a kid and got lost at the Arts and Entertainment Fair?"

She set her cup down and her forehead wrinkled in thought. I hoped my forehead didn't wrinkle like that when I got older. Other than the forehead thing though, I wouldn't mind looking like my mother at her age. The short pageboy haircut made her dark hair look shiny and her legs were hot for an old woman.

"Um...I think so. OH! Yes, the time I had my hands full of books and you were supposed to be holding onto my skirt. God, that was terrifying. I remember the moment I realized your grip was gone and then I turned around and you weren't there. My heart stopped. You probably shaved five years of my life off that day."

So it had been real. Mom's dark brown eyes peeped over the rim of her coffee cup as she took a sip. I wanted to ask more but the frown on her face stopped me. Her attention was fixed over my shoulder at the window. Dank was here. I hated her thinking my relationship with him had something to do with Leif disappearing. The fact was I'd never got a chance to break up with Leif. He'd vanished before I could. But telling her that would make things even worse. If I didn't know that Leif wasn't human then I'd be worried too but I knew the truth.

"I gotta go Mom. Love ya," I called out heading for the door. I didn't want to listen to her lecture me on being more concerned about the fact Leif had run away.

"It's almost time"

I stopped and stood frozen on the front steps of the house. My hand reached out and gripped the cold iron railing. I knew that voice.

"Pagan." Dank was in front of me instantly. Lifting my eyes to meet his I shook my head to clear it.

"Did you... did you see anyone or ...um, anything?" I stumbled through my words, still reeling from the voice spoken directly in my ear.

The blue color in Dank's eyes went from their normal brilliant blue to flickering orbs.

"Pagan, your eyes," he reached out and cupped my face with his hands as he studied me. Death wasn't supposed to fear anything; yet I could see it in every crease of his frown. The fact that his eyes looked like blue flames meant something.

"What about my eyes?" I asked in a panicked whisper.

Dank pulled me up against him tightly, "Come on, we're going."

I let him all but carry me to the Jeep and even put me inside and buckle me up.

"Dank, tell me what's wrong," I pleaded as he kissed me softly on the lips.

"Nothing. Nothing that I can't fix," he assured me and pressed his forehead to mine. "Listen to me Pagan, you have no reason to worry. I've got this. Remember what I told you. What Death protects can't be harmed and baby," the pad of his thumb caressed my cheek, "you're the only thing I protect."

The shivers I never seemed to be able to control when his voice dropped an octave and went all smooth and sexy seemed to make him happy. He always gave me a sexy smirk when I shivered.

"Okay, but I heard a voice. In my ear. Like when you talk to me but you're far away."

Dank tensed and he took a deep breath. "You did?"

I nodded and watched as he closed his eyes tightly and an angry snarl vibrated against his chest.

"No one gets that close to you. No *thing* gets that close to you." He kissed the tip of my nose and then closed the door before appearing in the driver's seat beside me. I sure hoped he wasn't so otherwise occupied that he wasn't paying attention to what my mother was doing. If she was looking out the window just now then things could get complicated.

"She's already closed off in her room writing," Dank said as he cranked the Jeep and pulled out onto the road. I didn't ask how he knew what I was thinking. I was used to this by now. I couldn't worry about anything without him knowing. He was obsessed with fixing all my problems. Normally that would frustrate me but right now with the problems I had looming I needed him.

"What did the voice say?" His voice was tense and I could tell he was trying to control the angry hiss that amused me when it was brought on because of jealousy. Right now it wasn't amusing. At all.

"It's almost time," I replied, studying his reaction. His left hand tightened on the steering wheel as he reached over and rested his hand on my thigh.

"I'll have this handled immediately. I didn't see anything but I felt it. The moment you froze, I felt it. It isn't a soul. It isn't a deity. It is nothing that I'm familiar with but that leaves only a few things it can be. And I promise you Pagan that not one of those things is a match for me. So stop worrying. I'm Death, baby. Remember that."

I let out a sigh and covered his hand with mine.

"I know," I replied and began tracing hearts on his hand with the tip of my finger.

"I missed you last night," he whispered in a husky voice.

I smiled down at his hands as he flipped it over and clasped mine in his. I liked knowing he missed me.

"Good."

An amused chuckle was his response.

CHAPTER TWO

When Dank pulled into the parking lot of the school, I did my daily check for Leif's truck. And just as the days before it was missing from his spot. Instead of someone taking the coveted parking slip of the most popular guy at school it remained empty. It was as if they were all waiting. Wondering.

The last time I'd seen Leif was the day I'd thought Dank was lost to me forever. Gee, a transporter who was trying to kill my body and force Death's hand, yet oddly enough became my friend, had managed to get my soul out of my body without Death's help. Problem was, it was too late. Death had already broken the rules and he had to pay for it. I was left with the decision to either become a lost wandering soul or get back in my body and live. Even though the only guy I'd ever love was burning in Hell like a fallen angel for not doing his job when it was time to take my life. Gee explained that Dank would be tormented even more in the pits of Hell if he knew I was a lost soul. He'd want to know that I lived. That his sacrifice was for something. I'd do anything to ease his pain. I got back in my body that morning and chose life. For him.

Then he'd been at school that morning and I hadn't even taken a moment to speak to Leif and explain. I'd just run to Dank. After Dank explained everything and then laid the whopper on me that Leif wasn't human we'd gone to find him. But Leif Montgomery was missing. That was a month ago.

"Don't frown," Dank's voice broke into my thoughts as his hand cupped my face and studied me. He could hear my fears. There was no reason to explain my sudden mood change.

"Will he ever come back?"

Dank let out a sigh while glancing back over my shoulder, "I'm afraid so."

"Why does that seem to bother you? I know you say Leif has no soul but I know Leif. I've spent time with him. He isn't evil. He's incredibly sweet."

Those blue eyes I loved lit up and the glow I was growing accustomed to warned me I'd said the wrong thing. Dank wasn't dealing well with the emotion of jealousy. It was completely new to him and it wasn't something he had a handle on.

"Leif is what he must be. He was created Pagan. He did his job. He isn't *sweet*. He has no soul.*"

I leaned forward and kissed his jaw then whispered, "Easy, big guy. We both know who owns my soul."

"That's right," Dank replied then nipped at my ear, "and don't you forget it."

I shivered from his warm breath against my skin.

Banging on my window startled me and I pulled back from my sexy boyfriend and turned to see

Miranda, my best friend, staring at me through the window with an amused expression.

"Saved by the best friend," Dank murmured pressing one last kiss to my neck before reaching for my backpack and opening his car door. He stepped out into the morning sunlight looking like a greek god. The jeans that hung perfectly from his hips cupped his butt deliciously. And Dank could rock a fitted t-shirt and did so on a daily basis. Today the t-shirt showing off his impressive chest was a dark blue. His black boots never changed but I liked them. They were all kinds of sexy. He looked like a bad ass even with my red backpack thrown over his left shoulder. I watched in helpless fascination as he sauntered around the front of his Jeep to open my door. I'd learned the hard way not to open my own car door. He didn't like it. I could feel Miranda's eyes on me but I didn't care. She could watch me ogle my boyfriend. Besides, she completely understood. Miranda thought, like the rest of the world, that Dank Walker was the lead singer of the rock band Cold Soul. Ironic, I know. Dank did sing with the band but he wasn't with them often. Miranda was a total fan girl.

Dank opened my door and I stepped out finally tearing my eyes off him to meet my friend's gaze.

"Well, good morning to you too," Miranda teased, slipping her arm in mine. "I wondered how long it was going to take you to stop staring at your rocker boyfriend like a worshipful puppy dog and notice little 'ol me."

I elbowed her, "shut up."

She giggled, "girl please tell me you aren't trying to be subtle with your lustful looks because you have failed. That boy knows you want his body."

"Stop it," I hissed

Dank came up behind me causing my insides to go all warm and tingly. "She can't possibly want my body more than I want hers."

Miranda began fanning herself with her hand, "Dear Lord, have mercy, I think I may swoon."

Dank's hand covered mine and he squeezed. "I'll meet you inside. I'm going to take these to your locker."

He was always so good about giving me time with Miranda. I nodded, not even caring that I had a goofy grin on my face.

Miranda slid her sunglasses up and rested them on top of her head. Her curls were styled perfectly which I knew from experience took her hours to do. The girl slept in rollers like it was 1980 or something. Her brown eyes twinkled as she watched my boyfriend's butt as he made his way inside the school.

"That is one fine piece of--"

"Miranda!" I shoved her with a grin because of course she was right. But still she didn't have to say it out loud.

"Jealous much?" she teased.

I only rolled my eyes.

Miranda's gaze drifted over to Leif's empty parking space. I couldn't explain to Miranda about Leif. She didn't even know I saw dead people, or as Dank liked to put it, 'wandering souls'. Until Dank, I'd had to live with my secret.

"I wonder where he is?"

When Leif had gone missing Dank and I decided to lay low with our relationship. It wasn't until just last week we'd started being out in the open with it. When the authorities and Leif's parents had questioned me I had told both of them that Leif and I had just broken up. That it was his decision. Which wasn't a total lie; he did vanish without a trace. That's is a form of breaking things off. At first his parents called on a daily basis to ask me if I'd heard from him. They stopped after Leif called and assured them he was fine. Apparently, he'd said he needed time away to deal with some issues. Strangely after that call his parents had seemed to be completely at ease with his disappearance. They no longer came around. I'd even seen his mother in the grocery store last week and she'd smiled brightly at me as if she didn't have a care in the world. Kids at school were slowly doing the same thing. No one brought him up much anymore. It was... weird.

"So, did you study for that trig test?" Miranda asked smiling, as if she hadn't just been worrying about Leif. Again.. weird.

"Yep. Until late last night."

Miranda groaned and flipped her hair over her shoulder. It was one of her dramatic mannerisms that made me laugh.

"If I fail my parents are going to lock me away in the attic for life. You'll have to come slip me food under the door."

"I doubt it will be all that bad. Besides you did study, right?"

She rolled her eyes over and glanced at me, "A little. Yeah."

"You watched *Pretty Little Liars* last night didn't you?"

With a deep sigh that caused her shoulders to move up and down she replied, "Yep. Last week's show and this week's. I can't help it. I have a thing for Caleb."

Grabbing her arm, I pull her inside. "Come on. To the library. We have thirty minutes and you're not going to get locked up in an attic for life."

Miranda beamed at me, "I love you."

"Ditto."

Hopefully, the library ghost would be somewhere else today. The soul who always wandered around in there was distracting.

Dank

I watched as Pagan led Miranda up to the library. She'd be busy for awhile and I had somewhere I needed to be. There was a soul I didn't want to leave waiting for me. I needed to be there for this one's actual death. Once Pagan entered the library and I knew she was safe for the time being, I left.

Before Pagan, I hadn't understood love. Before Pagan, taking souls had been easy. Now, I knew emotion. I knew pain and the feeling of loss and it made my purpose harder. Especially with the young ones. Even though I knew they'd get another life soon enough I understood their family's pain as they lost someone they held dear. Because although the soul of that child would return it wouldn't be the same. They wouldn't know the child they loved was once again with them when the soul returned in a new life.

"It's time, isn't it?" the little boy looked up at me as I entered his hospital room. I'd been to talk to him before. Several times actually. I wanted him to understand he would be dying soon but that if he followed my directions then he'd be given another life. His soul would live on. This life would just end. His bottom lip quivered as he stared up at me.

"Yeah, it's time."

"Will it hurt?"

I shook my head, "I promised you it wouldn't, didn't I?"

He nodded and pulled the dark green dinosaur closer against his chest tucking it under his chin. It had been a week since I'd last been here. His face was more drawn and the circles under his eyes were darker. The sickness was taking over.

"Mommy thinks I'm going to get better. I tried to tell her I wasn't."

The tightness in my chest appeared. This used to be so easy.

"Those who love you don't want to accept that your body in this life has grown too sick to continue. But remember: you'll come back. You'll be born into a new body and you will return to this family. Maybe not tomorrow or the next day but one day you'll return."

He sniffed and rubbed his nose against the stuffed animal he obviously loved.

"Yeah, but you said I wouldn't remember this life. I'd forget who I once was. I don't want to forget Mommy and Daddy. I don't want to forget Jessi, even if she can be mean sometimes, she's my big sister."

This was why Death wasn't meant to feel emotion. I wanted to cuddle the kid up in my arms and make false promises. Anything to ease his fear but this was his fate. He'd be back soon. I'd already asked about his soul after meeting him the first time. His sister was sixteen. In six years she'd give birth to a baby boy who'd she name after her brother and this soul would return.

"I know but you have to trust me. This is the way life works. You may not remember this life but your soul will always be attached to the ones you love. Your soul will be happy and although you won't remember, your soul will feel like it's come home."

The little boy nodded and set the dinosaur down. "Mommy just left to get me some ice. Can we wait until she comes back? I want to tell her bye," he choked on that last word.

I nodded and stood back as the door to his room opened. In walked his mother. She was also thinner since my last visit and the sorrow and fear rolling off her was breathtaking. The dark circles under her eyes looked almost as if she were the one dying today.

"Sorry it took so long, baby. I had to go to the next floor to get the ice you like," she hurried to his side. The wrinkled clothes hung on her frail frame. She was already grieving. She knew. She may have told her son he was going to get better but she knew.

"Mommy," his weak voice said with more strength than I expected. I watched as the small child reached for his mother's hand. He was about to comfort her. His body might be young but his soul wasn't. He had an old soul. One that had seen many lives. At the moment of death the soul began to take over. Even though his mind was that of a five year old his soul knew that his mother needed him to be strong right now.

"I love you," he said and a sob rattled her body. I wanted to hug her to help ease her pain but I couldn't. Death wasn't meant to comfort.

"I love you too sweet boy," she whispered squeezing his small hand in hers.

"I'll never really go away okay. Don't be sad."

He tried as so many others had to explain to the ones they were leaving behind that they would return. But like all humans she began weeping and shaking her head in denial. Facing the loss of her little boy was too much for her mind to comprehend.

"Don't talk like that baby. We're going to fight this," she said with a fierceness only a desperate mother could muster at a time like this.

"No mommy. I need to go now but I promise, I'll always be here."

I stepped up beside him as his mother covered his small body with hers. His small hand reached out to mine and I grasped it. He nodded and I took his soul.

"You always summon me for the tough ones. Why is that? Hmmmm? Cause your girlfriend likes me so you're getting back at me?" Gee grumbled as she strutted into the hospital room.

"This isn't about you Gee. It's about the kid. Take his soul now. He doesn't need to see the rest. He needs to go on up."

Gee glanced down at the mother weeping over the body that had once housed the soul. Her sobs were getting more intense and the nurses began rushing into the room shouting. Immediately Gee took the soul's hand and left without another word. She might be a pain in my ass but she wasn't heartless. That's why I always sent for her when it was a death like this one. With one last glance back at the grieving mother I left the room. She'd love her grandson one day and hold him close to her as she told him all about his uncle. The soul might not remember that life but he'd know what a fighter his uncle had been and that the life he'd only experienced for a short time would never be forgotten. His next life he'd grow old with his own grandchildren to tell stories to.

CHAPTER THREE

"Hey," Pagan murmured in her soft, sexy, sweet tone that meant she missed me.

Normally I didn't leave during the day to take souls. Only the tough ones or ones I'd made a connection with. I didn't have to be there for a body to die. I just had to be there to take the soul attached to it away from the body. So, although people died every second of every day I wasn't always there at that moment. It's why people often saw the "ghost" of their loved ones hours after their death. The soul stayed with the body until I came for it. Then there were the souls who refused to go. The ones who wouldn't leave. The ones who became lost souls and wandered the earth for all eternity confused.

"You look...sad," she pointed, out wrapping her arms around my waist.

"Just thinking," I assured her, pulling her tightly against my chest.

"You just took a soul, didn't you?" she replied, studying me.

I nodded.

"A kid?"

I nodded again, "a boy."

She understood. We'd talked about this before. There were so many things she'd wanted to know and I was helpless where she was concerned. I couldn't manage to tell the girl no.

"When will he come back?"

"In six years."

"Who took him?"

"Gee."

"Oh, good. He'll like her."

I grinned. Gee wasn't the most likable being I'd ever met but for some strange reason Pagan liked her. Even when she'd thought Gee was a teenage girl who suffered from schizophrenia.

She laid her head against my chest and sighed. Death wasn't something Pagan dealt with well but she was learning to understand it more.

Pagan

The tree wasn't so big. Stupid Wyatt didn't know nothing. Just because I was a girl didn't mean I couldn't climb it too. I'd show him. By the time he got here I'd be all the way at the top. See if he thinks girls can't do things boys can do. HA! We can do them better. Cause we're just cooler.

Glancing back to see if Mom was watching from the kitchen window and finding it all clear I grabbed a hold of the rough bark. It was warm and sticky. Once I had both arms and legs wrapped firmly around it I began inching myself up higher. I just wouldn't look down. I'd keep making my way until I was at the tippy top. No reason to look down. That would just mess me up. A sliver of wood cut into my hand and I yelped pulling it back to see if I was bleeding. There was a small splinter poking out of my hand and I pressed my palm against my mouth and used my teeth to pull it out. Smiling with satisfaction once the small painful bark was firmly between my teeth I jerked it out and spit the offending object out.

See, I was as tough as any boy. Wyatt and his dumb mouth saying I was weak. Whatever! I continued my upward climb. Maybe once he saw how much cooler I was than him because I could climb higher he'd let me into his new treehouse. That "boys only" sign looked just plain stupid anyway. Mom said I needed to ignore them and let the boys have their special hideout but I couldn't do that. It just wasn't fair when I was the one who came up with the treehouse idea in the first place. Besides, all Miranda wanted to do was put on makeup and paint our nails. Who wanted to waste time doing that stuff? Not me! That's who.

My foot slipped and I tightened my hold on the trunk trying not to panic. I could do this. My hands began to sweat and my firm grasp had weakened. This wasn't good. I moved my arm so I could find something to hold onto other than the tree trunk when my other foot slipped and I went into a free fall backwards. I tried to scream but nothing came out. Closing my eyes tightly I waited for the ground to slam into my back. It was going to hurt.

"Umph, got you," a familiar voice said and I opened my eyes to see a boy staring down at me. He was holding me. Odd. Shaking my head I stared up at the tree I'd just fallen from and tried to remember

how I knew this boy. Had I hit my head and he picked me up?

"Uh," I replied still confused. I'd been falling. Then... this boy was holding me and talking.

"What were you doing up there? That was too high."

I turned my gaze back to his, "Um, I uh... did you catch me?" I asked incredulously.

He grinned and the light blue color of his eyes appeared to darken. "Yeah. Why else do you think you're not lying on the ground with a few broken bones?"

I shook my head and pushed to stand up. He put me down easily and once again I was startled by how familiar he looked. Did he go to school with us?

"Where'd you come from?"

He shrugged, "Just around. Saw you climbing too high and came over to see if you needed help."

"Do I know you?" I asked watching his face take on a strange smile.

"I wish you did but you don't. Not yet. It isn't time."

"What do you mean?"

He was weird and he talked like a grown up.

"Pagan Moore, get your butt over here if you're going to get a sneak peek at my tree house before the boys get here," Wyatt was standing at the street grinning at me like he'd just offered me a million dollars.

What was he talking about a "peek?" I wanted IN. Not a stupid peek. I glanced back at the

34

boy who'd caught me to see if he wanted to come too but he was gone.

"Almost time, almost time, almost time, almost time."

I sat up in bed gasping for breath as the chanting in my ear faded away. The same voice from yesterday. I knew that voice. Didn't I? And what did it mean by "almost time."

I dropped my head into my hands and sighed. What was happening to me? These dreams seemed so real. Like memories I'd forgotten. The same boy. The same voice.

I stared through my fingers at the light barely coming through my window. The sun wasn't even completely up yet. There was no way I was going back to sleep. Mom would be thrilled I'd managed to get up in time to eat breakfast with her today. The dream was going to bother me. I needed to ask Wyatt about that tree. Had I told him about falling? I couldn't remember. Maybe he would.

Getting out of bed I brushed my hair and stood at my window studying the old oak tree. It felt like there was another memory attached to that tree but I couldn't quite remember it. I put the brush down and slipped on my flip flops and made my way outside. I wanted to go out there. It was almost as if the tree suddenly had some sort of invisible pull to it.

The cool morning air caused me to shiver as I walked down the porch steps and across the damp grass. A jacket would have been a wise decision but I'd been too anxious to come see this tree.

Scanning the yard for anything odd or strange, I walked over to the tree. It was the same as it had always been. Never really changed. Except maybe that bottom branch was now easier to reach. I studied the spot on the tree I remember reaching before I fell and calculated how far I actually fell. Could a boy actually catch me and not fall down himself from the impact? That just seemed highly unlikely.

Dank

She was scared. I could feel it even though I was a continent away. Glancing back at Gee I frowned because we weren't finished. I still had eight hundred more souls to collect before I could call it a day.

"We need to hurry," I snapped turning to leave the stubborn soul who wasn't willing to leave.

"Wait, aren't you going to help me convince this one to go? I mean, come on lover boy, I know you want to get back to your woman and all but we have a job to do."

"And this one is being stubborn. Let it wander the earth for eternity if that's what it wants. I've tried."

Gee frowned and closed the distance between us, "Is she okay? I can go. You can summon someone else to --"

"No. She needs me. Let's go. This one is a lost cause."

"UGH! You're so freaking impatient," Gee fired back at me.

"I don't have time for this. Take the soul or leave it. I don't care." The need to get to Pagan was consuming me. I couldn't concentrate. "Do what you can with this one. I'll meet you at the next stop. I've got to check on her." I didn't wait for Gee's reply.

She stood outside in her back yard staring up at an old oak tree. Her hair was hanging down her back in soft freshly brushed waves which looked out of place with her pajama bottoms and tank top.

"You okay?" I asked closing in behind her to wrap her up in my arms. She didn't even startle anymore. My appearing out of nowhere had become normal for her. The thought made me smile but her worry wiped the smile off my face quickly. Something was bothering her.

"Why are you outside so early looking at a tree?" I asked resting my chin on the top of her head.

"I had a dream. It wasn't the first one. I think... I think they have something to do with that voice."

Tightening my hold on her I scanned the yard in the early morning light. Nothing was out here but the two of us. She was safe, I reminded myself.

"Tell me about the dreams," I encouraged.

She lay her hands over mine and let her head fall back on my shoulder.

"They're all memories from my childhood. Memories I've forgotten. In each one there is this boy.

The same one. He always helps me. I didn't remember him until the dreams started but now I think they're real memories. Not just dreams. I can remember them so clearly it's as if I'm there," she paused and pointed to the tree in front of us. " T h a t tree, I climbed it once. I was mad because Wyatt said I couldn't do it because I was a girl. I wanted to prove him wrong. I climbed it but I, I fell... and he caught me."

"Wyatt?"

She shook her head, "No. The boy. He helped me find my mother in a crowd when I got lost and there are other times. I've seen him. I know him."

The angry jealous snarl escaped me before I could stop it.

Pagan jerked around in my arms to frown up at me, " what?"

I shook my head and took a deep breath. This wasn't an emotion I was good with just yet. I was beginning to wonder if I ever would be. I was selfish and possessive. Pagan was mine.

"You believe he's real?" I managed to ask. I needed to keep focused on the issue at hand. I hated knowing someone else had saved her as a child. It didn't set well with me. Something was off. She'd forgotten and now the memories were back. The voice. I needed to find this voice.

"Yes. I think the boy is the voice in my ear," she squeezed my arms, "stop snarling Dank. You're not an animal. Jeez."

She was right of course. But I was angry. The possessive need to claim her as mine was overwhelming. This voice was too close to her if he was getting in her dreams. It was the night time while I was away that he got close to her. I'd have to change that. No more dreams. I would just need to be gone more during the day. I hated being away from her when she was awake. But I was left without much of a choice. This... this thing was too close to her.

"I'm not going to leave you at night anymore. Not until I've ended this."

Pagan frowned and shook her head, "No. I don't want you to be gone during the day. I'll miss you."

I'd miss her too. "I don't like him being that close to you. He's getting in your head at night because I'm not there to feel him. To stop him."

She chewed on her bottom lip and studied my chest a moment then finally looked back up at me.

"What about Gee?"

"What about her?"

"She could stay with me. For right now."

She could. She wouldn't be crazy about it but then Gee liked Pagan as much as Pagan liked Gee. I could trust Gee to get me if Pagan needed me.

"I'll talk to Gee."

Pagan beamed at me and wrapped her arms around my neck.

"You're so easy. I hardly ever have to argue with you."

I kissed the tip of her nose, "I like making you smile Pagan."

"And I like hearing your sexy voice say sweet things to me," she replied.

"Kiss me Dank," she whispered, pressing her lips against mine. This wasn't something I encouraged. The few times we'd kissed her soul had tried to release from her body. I couldn't seem to figure out how to stop that. Our kisses were always short. Now, other things... we spent time doing those other things.

"Hmmm... you think you can hold onto your soul this time?" I murmured against her lips.

She giggled, "I'll try."

The taste of her sweet tongue sent all other thoughts far from my mind. Instantly, I had one need. One purpose. Pagan. Satisfaction seeped through me as I ran my tongue across her bottom lip fighting the urge to bite it. The plump swell always tempted me. A soft little moan brought me back to my senses and I felt her soul began to react to the draw she felt toward me. Gently, I broke the kiss and put distance between the two of us while we stood staring hungrily at each other and taking very fast short breaths.

"Sorry," she whispered.

Shaking my head, I smiled at her innocent apology. Her soul knew it was mine. The fact that she was so willing to surrender it was actually precious to me. Even though it caused extreme frustration when I wanted to wrap her in my arms and kiss her senseless

40

for hours at a time. Until we found an answer to her soul's draw towards me, that wouldn't be happening.

"Don't apologize, Pagan," I replied, reaching out to take her hand and bring it to my lips. "It's time for you to go inside and get ready. I believe you promised your mother you'd sit down for breakfast this morning."

She nodded and squeezed my hand before turning around and heading inside. As she reached the door she glanced back at me. "I'll see you soon."

"Always," I replied.

CHAPTER FOUR

The second she stepped inside and closed the door I felt it. I closed my eyes and let my senses take over. Slowly opening them I scanned the backyard until my eyes landed on the source of Pagan's dreams. I'd seen this spirit before. The mocking cold gleam in his eyes stared back at me, while he pulled out not one but two cigarettes that hung from his mouth.

"What do you want with Pagan?" I demanded, holding it in place with my glare. The spirit lord might be able to manipulate humans and their lives but it had no power over me. I held all the keys. Without me the voodoo spirit lord of the dead would be nothing. His powers came from those who believed in him. It ended at my hands.

"She belongs to me." The arrogant spirit kept his focus on me. I could see the caution in his black eyes. He knew he was outranked.

"No. She doesn't."

The spirit lord moved backward. His movement was more of a slither than a walk as he put distance between us. The growl in my chest met my ears and I understood his sudden need for space.

"De gurl is marked as a restitution. Her mama made de deal. She know de cos."

What? Unwilling to tear my eyes from the spirit lord and check to see if Pagan was watching us from her window, I negated the attempt at putting distance between us and glowered coldly into the eyes of what could only be considered a demon to humans. The worship and belief of those who practiced Voodoo was the place he drew his only power. Without them, he wouldn't exist.

"Pagan Moore is mine. Leave her alone. You've never crossed me before but I can assure you that a voodoo spirit lord is no match for me. You know this."

The rattle in the voodoo spirit lord's composure was evident. He backed up. "But de restitution mus be made."

"NOT with Pagan it doesn't. Whatever deal you had with her mother is with her mother. Pagan had nothing to do with this."

"You'd of never known her if I hadn't healed her. You'd of taken her soul whilst she lay curled up dying as a child. It's me who don lak to see chilren die. You don care who you take. She's alive because of me. She's meant for me purpose. I saved her for me son. He's watched over her all dese years."

Shaking with rage, I controlled my need to cause destruction. If I attempted to annihilate a voodoo spirit lord in Pagan's backyard it would bring all of Hell with it. This was to be a safe place for her. Not a place of nightmares.

"Leave her or deal with me."

"De gurl wilt have to choose or ahm taking my payment in udder forms. I got de right," he hissed.

"Fine! Let her choose," I roared.

Then he was gone and I stood alone.

What in the name of all the deities had Pagan's mother done?

Pagan

"So lover boy's on tour," Wyatt, Miranda's boyfriend and my childhood friend, announced as he st his tray down on the table in front of me. I picked up the roll because it was the only thing on the tray I actually recognized and pinched off a piece before peering up at him.

"Yeah," was my only response before popping the chunk of bread into my mouth.

"Don't talk about it. She's all depressed," Miranda scolded, slapping at his arm.

Wyatt continued to watch me which was slightly unnerving.

"What?" I asked, meeting his stare.

He shrugged, "Nothing, I was just thinking about something and I was going to ask you about it and well.. I forgot." He shook his head as if to clear it and grabbed his bottle of water.

Leif. He'd been thinking about Leif. Slowly Leif was fading from everyone's memory. Everyone but mine of course. Why was that?

"Wyatt, do you remember the tree house you built and wouldn't let girls into?"

Wyatt lifted his gaze from his food and grinned at me, "Yeah and you were so freaking mad. I think I hung that sign just to piss you off."

I was sure he did. Wyatt had lived to make me mad. We had a huge boy versus girl battle going back then. Miranda was happy to play with her Bratz dolls which just gave him more ammunition. Miranda made me look bad. Dolls made the boys think we were weak and I was so not weak.

"Do you remember the tree in my backyard you climbed and said I couldn't?"

Wyatt frowned a minute and then a grin broke across his face, "YES and you did climb it one day by yourself and fell down but a kid helped you or something. I don't know. I didn't believe your story then and I don't believe it now. It was a little far fetched," he continued to go on and on about how fast he could climb that tree and his obvious prowess where it was concerned but my mind was on other things.

The boy had been real. That dream was a memory. Why had I forgotten it?

"You gonna eat that?" Wyatt's question broke into my thoughts and I pushed my tray toward him. I wasn't sure what "that" he was referring to but all the "thats" on my plate weren't going anywhere near my mouth.

"Help yourself."

"Sweet. Thanks," he grabbed the tray and pulled it in front of him.

Miranda shivered as she stared down at it. That had been my thought exactly.

"So Pagan, when are we going to get to double with you and Dank?"

"Um... I don't know. I didn't know you wanted to."

Miranda cocked her head to one side and gave me an incredulous look, "Of course we want to. You've been the one holding out."

No. Wyatt was friends with Leif. Wyatt hadn't been crazy about Dank and me. He felt like I was cheating on Leif even though I'd told them all that Leif had broken up with me. I shifted my gaze to Wyatt who was happily eating the food I'd given him while waiting on me to reply. Had they forgotten Leif completely?

"Oh, okay, well let me talk to him. He'll be gone for a little while but when he gets back, then sure."

Wyatt grinned and took a swig of water. I shifted my attention to the table beside us where Leif normally sat as reigning king. No one seemed to be concerned about his absence. Not even Kendra, his girlfriend for years before he'd broken things off with her this summer. Had they ever really been a couple or had he just played with her head?

Kendra threw her head back and laughed at something one of the boys said and I watched in fascination as she flirted openly with them. Thankfully she'd forgotten all about Dank once he left the first time. I hadn't had to deal with her flirting with him on his return. It was almost like I didn't exist as far as she was concerned. Then her eyes caught mine and a flicker of knowledge startled me before she gazed right past me and squealed out the name of another cheerleader approaching the table. They all acted like nothing had happened. No one worried over their star quarterback anymore.

"I need to brush my teeth and reapply lipstick. Come with?" Miranda asked, standing up.

I nodded and stood up to follow her out of the cafeteria.

"Hey Miranda, so Wyatt's not upset about Leif so much now," I coaxed, waiting to see how she responded.

Miranda peered back over her shoulder, "Who?"

Mom wasn't home. Fantastic. I was alone. I closed the door behind me and scanned the kitchen to see if there were any unwanted visitors either floating around or, in Leif's case, walking around. The coast seemed clear but that didn't calm my nerves much. I dropped my bag on the table and walked over to the fridge to get a drink and make myself a sandwich.

A taco salad complete with a crispy tortilla bowl was wrapped up with a sticky note on top.

Gone out with Roger. Be back late. I ordered your favorite from Los Tacos. Enjoy.

Love you,

Mom

Add this to the fact that she'd left me at home alone and I could kiss her face. I was starving after nothing but a roll for lunch. I'd tutored two freshmen after school and there had been no time for eating then. Now it was after six and I swear my big intestines were eating my little intestines. I needed food. Grabbing the salad and a can of soda I headed for the living room. After hearing Miranda talk about this week's *Pretty Little Liars*, I wanted to watch it myself.

Sinking down onto the couch with my meal I tucked my feet up under me and turned on the television. Thanks to good 'ol Roger, my mom's boyfriend, we had ourselves a nice new sixty-two inch flat screen on the wall. Roger was the district manager over the Best Buys in this area so he got killer deals. I'd already dropped the hint I was in the market for a new laptop. My old one was headed to the grave yard fast.

"Pagan."

Screaming, I dropped my fork and scanned the room for the owner of that voice.

Leif stood just inside the doorway leading into the kitchen. He didn't look ghostly or freaky. He just looked like Leif. Except he was in my house. Uninvited. And he didn't have a soul.

"Pagan," he repeated.

I opened my mouth to asked him what the

heck when he disappeared in front of me as Gee came storming in the door like she was on the warpath.

"Where is he? Where's that little shit at? I felt him. Now WHERE THE HELL ARE YOU?"

I watched as Gee scanned the living room and stalked into the kitchen. "He's gone. Freaking coward," she said out loud as she stormed up the steps.

I sat frozen waiting for Gee to calm down and come back into the room. I was still reeling over Leif being in my house and Gee was yelling curse words while she searched every corner.

"You okay?" she asked once she walked back into the room. I tried to nod but I couldn't manage. Instead, I forced a "mmm" out of my throat. My heart was still racing so fast it felt as if it was going to beat through my chest.

"Deep breaths, Peggy Ann. Take deep breaths. Don't get his majesty over here raining down hell on all who get in his path because his girl is scared shitless."

Her colorful vocabulary caused a giggle to erupt and I was able to take the deep breath she suggested.

"There we go. Good girl," she affirmed with a satisfied smile and sank down on the sofa beside me.

I stared down at the salad in my lap trying to work through my head the fact that Leif had been in my house. He'd just appeared out of nowhere. Had it been something else that looked like Leif? He'd sure sounded like Leif.

"You gonna eat that?" Her question sounded more like a demand as she motioned to the salad bowl that had miraculously not been spilled all over the floor during the drama.

I needed to eat it. I hadn't eaten all day but the hunger was gone. Now I felt slightly ill.

"That was Leif, right?" I asked turning my head so I could see her face.

"Yep. Little shit. Showing up like a damn coward and scaring you like that. Ain't so sweet now, is he?"

I glanced back over to where he'd been standing. He hadn't looked scary. He had looked worried. Or maybe guilty.

"Dank's gonna get this all worked out. Stop worrying. Now, you gonna eat that or not because it looks good."

I shook my head and Gee snatched it up and instantly a fork was in her hand.

"Sip on your drink if you feel sick. You don't want to go into shock. The sugar will help."

Nodding, I took a small sip of the cold sweet soda and my stomach seemed to settle some.

"Why was he here?"

"Cause he wanted to talk to you, I guess," Gee replied before shoving another forkful of salad into her mouth.

"The kids at school, his parents, they're all forgetting him."

Gee nodded, "Yeah they are. He didn't have a soul, Pagan. Remember, you are a soul. Your body is just the house for it. Those with souls will forget him because their souls were never attached to his. Can't be attached to something that isn't there."

"Why do I remember him?" My voice came out in a whisper. I was almost afraid to hear the answer to this one.

Gee set the fork down in her bowl and sighed. That wasn't good.

"You're different. He has... There is this... Ugh, why the hell didn't Dankmar explain this crazy shit to you?" Gee placed the almost empty tortilla bowl on the coffee table and broke off a piece of it before leaning back again and looking at me.

"Your soul was marked when you were a child. Leif has some sort of claim on your soul. Now, don't go getting all freaked out. Dank is more than able to fix this but until he does Leif will be linked to you."

I didn't like the sound of that. "Linked?" I choked out.

Gee nodded and took another bite of the broken tortilla bowl in her hand. She was handling all this so casually. Maybe I needed to calm down. She wasn't worried. But... linked?

"Stop frowning, Peggy Ann. It isn't all that bad. So, here's the deal: your mom made a bad decision. You have a dark spirit determined to claim you. Things could be worse," she finished with a shrug of her shoulders.

"How? How could they be worse? A dark spirit?" I reached for my soda as my stomach rolled at the thought of what a dark spirit actually meant.

"How could it be worse? Well, for starters, you could be without the complete devotion of Death himself. I mean, come on, Peggy Ann. What is one dark spirit up against Death? I mean, really." Gee rolled her eyes and popped the last bite, of the tortilla bowl she was holding, into her mouth.

I soaked in her words wishing they were more comforting.

"You got anything good recorded on this thing?" Gee asked, reaching for the remote control.

"Um, yes just watch whatever," I muttered and sipped at my drink wishing Dank would come home. Now.

CHAPTER FIVE

Pagan

"Please. If you can save her then just do it! Do whatever you have to," my mommy begged with tears streaming down her face.

The wrinkled old lady stared down at me. Her white hair stood out against her dark skin. She studied me carefully before lifting her glassy gaze back to my mother. "You axe me for gris-gris dat wilt cause tings you mightna want."

"Anything. I'm begging you, anything you can do. The doctors can't help her. She's dying. Anything, please," my mommy's voice broke as she let out a loud sob.

"Etel ne'er passe' tis you know," the old lady said as she hobbled over to a shelf with hundreds of containers filled with strange things I didn't recognize. "What you axe don matta. Ain't non udder way. If de beb he want ta live. He make dat call."

I watched as she shuffled around mixing different items she took off the shelf while she muttered to herself.

"Who is he?" I heard my mommy ask.

I had been wondering that myself. He seemed to be calling the shots not the old lady. Why Mommy was asking her to help me I didn't understand. She didn't look like any doctor I'd ever seen. When I'd fallen asleep the white walls of the hospital room I'd spent the last few months in were the last thing I remembered seeing. Then I woke up and I was here. With this strange woman in a small dirty house that smelled funny.

"De only one dat can save dis gurl," she said, shuffling over to me while she stirred the smelly concoction and began softly chanting.

"Where is he? Do I need to go get him?" The panic in mommy's voice made me fight to keep my eyes open. I knew she was scared. The doctors didn't expect me to wake up. I'd heard them whispering while they'd thought I was sleeping. The disease had taken over my body. I was sick. My mommy was sad.

"You tink I'd do dis iffn' he weren't here," the humor in the old lady's voice was obvious. "Dis gris-gris I don do. Only him."

Before mommy could ask any more questions the door opened and in stepped a boy not much older than me. His eyes reminded me of a stormy sea swirling wildly as he closed the door behind him. Blond shaggy hair hung in his eyes and he didn't look as if he belonged to the older dark lady. Was he sick too? A low murmur in a language I didn't understand tumbled out of his mouth as the room began to darken and my eyes slowly closed.

"It's time," the familiar voice whispered in my ear.

I sat straight up in bed gasping for air. Sunlight poured through my window and the bright cheeriness of my yellow room seemed at odds with the dark shack I'd been dreaming about. Where had that come from? And that old woman's accent. It had been thick and... and Cajun? Then there had been the boy. Once again he'd been there while I was sick. I had been sick. I'd had a miraculous recovery at the age of three. This memory of the boy was the earliest I'd had. Who was he? And why had the voice said "It's time" instead of "It's almost time"?

Glancing around the room I searched for Gee.

"Pagan," Dank was standing in front of my bed and bending down to pull me in his arms.

"Gee said he got to you. She couldn't see him but she felt him. She can't stop him so she came and got me."

I nodded, letting him fuss over me. It was a comfort measure I needed right now. None of this made sense.

"I remembered something. Another dream. It doesn't make sense but if it is real... then it explains something. Something from my past."

Dank pulled back and stared down at me.

"What?" the tightness in his voice didn't surprise me. He was upset.

"I was sick once. When I was little. Really sick. I had leukemia and the doctors had given my mom no hope... and... and then I was all better. It was a miracle. We never really spoke about it after that. Mom never worried it would return. The check-ups with my doctors ended a few years later and that was the end of it."

Dank's hold on me had turned into a vice-like grip. "What did you remember in your dreams?"

"It was so real, Dank. I could even smell the moldy scent of the old shack."

"Tell me," he encouraged, as his fingers ran through my tangled hair gently working out the knots as he went.

"An old lady was there. Her accent was thick. It was hard to understand everything she said. I'm not even sure what kind of accent it was. But she was doing a... spell, I think. Mom had taken me to her. She was begging her to save me. Then the boy, the one from the other dreams, he was there. He began chanting something and then... I woke up to the words 'it's time' being repeated in my ear."

Dank sighed and rested his forehead on mine. That wasn't reassuring.

"Do you understand this? Do you know what's happening to me? Is this because Leif has a claim on my soul?"

He didn't respond right away. Instead he cupped the back of my head with one hand and ducked his head into the curve of my neck. Although I enjoyed being all cuddled up to him on my bed his hesitancy to answer me was taking away from the warm cozies I normally felt in this position.

"Dank," I repeated.

"It was a Voodoo doctor that you visited that day Pagan. Your mother allowed evil magic to save your body."

What! I swallowed the bile in my throat. What was he talking about? Voodoo wasn't real but the fear overtaking my body told me it believed in Voodoo. It knew something I didn't.

"I don't understand," I managed to choke out over the gripping terror clogging my airways.

"I'm going to find a way to fix this. Evil has a claim on your soul. Deities don't associate with voodoo spirits. They aren't all powerful but they can use their power over humans to cause pain. A restitution must be made in order to send them away from you. I can protect you but the spirit after you is the most powerful voodoo spirit out there. It won't go away without a fight."

"Leif is a... a voodoo spirit?" That couldn't be right. Leif wasn't evil.

"Pagan, those who don't have souls can only belong to one place. The Creator does not create soulless creatures. He has no use for them. A soul can only be created by the Creator. Therefore, all that doesn't contain a soul is evil. Leif is the product of one of the strongest evil spirits there is. The Voodoo lord of the dead, Ghede, is powerful because of the chants and prayers he receives from humans. Leif is his creation. His child. Leif is the prince of the dead within the Voodoo religion. Your connection to him is the reason you see souls. Before you were sick, before your mother took you to the voodoo doctor, had you ever seen a soul?"

I couldn't remember. This was too much. Voodoo? My mother saved me with Voodoo? Oh God.

"How... how can you fix this?" I asked, needing someone to reassure me it was going to be okay. Maybe this was just another dream. Maybe I would wake up and I would be normal again.

Dank dropped his arms from around me and stood up. I didn't like the distance. I wanted him close.

"When I'm not taking souls I will be finding a way to end this," he paused then looked away from me, "Gee is going to come stay with you until I've handled this."

What? No!

"You mean you're leaving?" I fought the tears stinging my eyes and threatening to spill. I couldn't do this without him here. I wanted to be strong and fearless but right now I just needed him near me.

Dank let out a sigh and closed his eyes and ran his hand over his face. I knew I was making this hard on him but I didn't want him to go away. Even if I loved Gee, I wanted Dank.

"There is no other answer to this Pagan. I can't exactly forego my job. I still have to take souls. All my free time will to be focused on keeping you safe."

"But--"

"PAGAN! BREAKFAST!" my mother's voice rang up the stairs interrupting my attempt at begging.

"Go get ready Pagan. Go to school. I won't stay gone completely. Every chance I get I'll be right here."

"You promise?"

"Yes."

"Alright Peggy Ann, where we headed first?"

I turned to look at Gee who had fallen in step beside me, I realized she didn't look like an ethereal "transporter" but instead the Gee I'd met in the mental hospital. Her blond hair was spiky and bleached white. Her eyebrow was again pierced and it looked like she'd added another small bar beside it. The diamond in her nose was no doubt very real and, of course, she had to be wearing black lipstick. She made the wanna be goths look pathetic in their attempts to pull off the style.

"Whatcha staring at Peggy Ann? You miss me that much?"

"I'd forgotten how well you can pull off the crazy bad-ass look."

Gee burst into a cackle of laughter. "You said ass," Gee announced rather loudly causing me to wince a little. "My little princess is getting some bite to her."

Rolling my eyes I glanced past Gee to see Miranda standing by her locker with Wyatt watching me with a horrified expression on her face. She'd remember Gee from the crazy house. Crap. I hadn't thought of that.

"Um, my friend Miranda saw you... ya know before. What am I going to tell her?"

Gee followed my gaze and then waved at my friends as if they were long lost buddies of hers. "She isn't staring at me with her mouth hung open because she remembers me Pay-gan. She's gawking because I don't fit the profile you normally hang with."

I started to respond and decided not to. Gee was right. My friends didn't have piercings on their face, or wear short miniskirts with tall black army boots. Or deck themselves out in black nail polish and lipstick. Gee was definitely going to draw attention.

"So, she doesn't remember you from the mental house?"

Gee shook her head, "Nope, Dank took care of that."

With a sigh of relief I made my way over to Miranda. I wasn't up for telling more lies today. I was glad I wouldn't have to come up with something to appease Miranda's questions. Although, I was going to have to find a way to get Miranda to stop gaping at Gee like she had a third eyeball. Gee was really cute all dressed up like a rebel. Sure she was gorgeous when she was all transporty but she pulled this look off well too.

"Miranda, Wyatt, this is my friend Gee," then I was stumped. I hadn't thought that far.

Miranda's horrified slightly confused gaze shifted from me to Gee lingering just a little longer on Gee.

"Gee?" Miranda asked

"Yep, Gee. Look your friend can already say my name. Isn't she a bright one?" Gee teased, obviously eating up the uncomfortable gawking. I elbowed her hard in the ribs and shot a warning glare at her.

"Gee is a friend of mine from out of town. Her uh, Dad is a friend of my Mom and she's staying with me for a few weeks," I stumbled all over my words. If they believed me, then it would be a miracle.

"If this fascinating introduction is over, I'm going to go find a vending machine. I need a Coke and a Snickers since you rushed me out of the house before breakfast," Gee announced then headed off in what appeared to be the direction of the Teacher's Lounge. Surely she wouldn't. No, she probably would and was going to.

"So she has to *live* with you? Like in your house? Please tell me you lock your doors because she looks insane. Maybe you should just sleep with your mother. I mean, honestly Pagan, she has probably been in jail or," Miranda gasped and covered her mouth, "I bet she has. Ohmygod I so bet that is why she's here! What did she do? That is so unsafe--"

"Miranda, calm down," I interrupted her babbling and grabbed her arm. "She hasn't been in jail. She's harmless. She just likes to draw attention. Now stop making up insane scenarios and relax."

"She's kind of funky looking," Wyatt piped up. I shot him a "shut up" glare and hooked my arm in Miranda's.

"She's eccentric but she's fun. You'll love her once you get over her appearance and colorful language."

"Colorful language? Oh no, she curses a lot?"

I nodded, "Yep and it's amusing. She could put a sailor to shame."

"I like her already," Wyatt said glancing back to the corner where Gee had walked around. "You don't think she's going to the Teacher's Lounge do you? Because that's the only vending machine that way."

I sighed and tugged Miranda toward our first period class. "That's probably exactly where she's going."

"That's just badass," Wyatt replied in awe, then a very loud "umph, ow baby," followed. Miranda had gone for his ribs with her pointy little elbow.

I laughed for the first time all morning before I remembered Leif and the mark on my soul. My smile quickly faded.

CHAPTER SIX

Dank

"You know, I've been thinking," Gee said as she appeared beside me. I walked through the desert taking the souls from fallen soldiers. I hated wars. They took up a lot of my time.

"Ooo, you missed one," Gee pointed to the soul standing beside the body he'd once inhabited.

"I didn't forget one Gee. He doesn't want to leave," I snapped, annoyed that she was here when she was supposed to be with Pagan. "Why are you here?"

"Well hello to you too Dankmar, geez chill, Pagan is safely eating dinner at her friend Miranda's house. Miranda doesn't like me. I'm positive she's terrified of me and is waiting on me to drink blood or something."

I snorted, "Ya think? Try to look less scary."

"Whatever, listen, why is it that you can't just go say 'Yo, stop haunting my girl you stupid ass piece of shit' and then be done with it? I realize you're hanging with the humans these days but Dank, you're Death. What's with all this angst?"

I finished with the last soul and then we were walking down the smoke covered highway into a pileup of cars that had just happened. Ambulances were just arriving and the traffic was backed up for miles.

"I can't just tell a Voodoo spirit to stop and expect them to stop. I have no control over a Voodoo spirit lord. His power comes from humans. It's an evil spirit. Not a human soul."

Gee sighed, "This is ridiculous. What the hell did her mother do?"

Jaslyn, another transporter, appeared and I sent the souls taken from the wreck to her and she waved at Gee before vanishing.

Then we were inside the house of another celebrity. America would mourn this in the morning. But unfortunately, this was a regular occurrence. The pill bottle lay open and empty beside the bed and the soul came out looking confused. I turned to Gee, "Take this one, then get back to Pagan. I'm almost done and you're just slowing me down."

Gee snarled and beckoned the soul before they both vanished. Thankfully. I needed some peace and quiet. Besides, I had hospitals left to visit.

Pagan

Gee hadn't wanted to hang around and eat at Miranda's. Which was probably a good thing since she would have scared Miranda's mother senseless. I was reaching to open my car door when suddenly the hairs on my arms stood up. Glancing up at Miranda's front door I thought about sprinting back to it and rushing inside. But my feet felt heavy. Whatever was here wasn't going to let me get away that easily. Where was Gee when I needed her?

"It's just me, Pagan," Leif's voice surprised me and I managed to slowly turn around. Sure enough. It was Leif. Looking as normal as when he had been standing in my kitchen doorway. But he wasn't normal. My body hair standing at attention proved he wasn't normal. He'd never caused that to happen before. Was it because I now *knew* what he was?

"Leif?" I croaked out, waiting to see if the boy I'd trusted would morph into some strange demon before my eyes. God, I hoped not.

"Can we talk?"

That would be a bad idea. Voodoo wasn't cool. And I was positive their spirit prince of the dead wasn't either. Where was Gee and what did I do about this?

"Um... well... you kind of scare the crap out of me so I'm not sure I want that."

He chuckled and I almost relaxed. I was familiar with that sound. Leif's chuckle always made me smile.

"There's nothing to be scared of. I would never hurt you."

I rubbed at the hairs on my arms thinking that my body begged to differ and he shrugged, "That I can't help. Not anymore. I'm not in a human form any longer. You're going to react to me that way."

Human form? Any longer?

"What do you want?"

He took a step toward me and I pressed up against the door of my car. The cool metal did

67

nothing to soothe the strange heat coming off his body.

"Hmm... I should have guessed you'd ask that question first. You always cut to the chase," he flashed the crooked grin I'd always loved. "But I need you to trust me and listen."

Trust him? Not likely.

"Have I ever hurt you Pagan?"

Well... not exactly. I responded only with a small shake of my head.

"And I never will. Haven't I always been there when you needed me? The tree, the lake, the time you were lost... the time you were dying from the disease in your body."

Realization washed over me and I stared at him. His baby blue eyes. The shape of his jaw. His posture. The curve of his lips and sound of his voice. He -- Leif was -- he was the boy from my dreams.

"It's you."

A regular guy would need clarification from my simple statement but Leif wasn't regular. He understood what I meant. So instead, he simply nodded.

"Why? I don't understand."

"You were promised to me. My father's power healed you and in return your mother promised your soul to me."

I was obviously dreaming again because this sounded ridiculous.

"I see it in your eyes," his grin grew larger, "your soul knows me. The fire is there." He held up a mirror which came out of nowhere and I stared in horror as my eyes were no longer their familiar green but instead were the color of fire. My pupils were surrounded by what looked like flickering orange flames.

Trembling, I shook my head and pushed away from the car to put more distance between us.

"Pagan--" he started then his face turned furious as he tilted his head upward and was once again gone.

"I missed him again, didn't I? Well, shit!" Gee hissed.

I sagged against the bumper of my car and wrapped my arms around my waist.

"You okay? He didn't touch you did he?"

I turned my face up to look at Gee and she stiffened, staring directly into my eyes.

"Your eyes," she said reaching out and touching my cheek carefully. "What the fuck?"

I shook my head and stood up turning away from her. I needed Dank. This was bad. My eyes were beyond creepy.

"Where's Dank?" I croaked, not wanting to cry in front of Gee. She wasn't the kind of being you wanted to get emotional in front of.

"Get in the car, I'll drive." Gee commanded, nodding her head to the passenger side. Normally, I wouldn't be okay with her driving because everything Gee did she did dangerously but at the moment I couldn't concentrate enough to drive. So I did as I was told and sank down into the passenger seat.

"Where's Dank?" I repeated as she cranked the car and backed up entirely too fast out of the driveway.

"In Afghanistan dealing with those idiots who blow themselves up."

"When will he be back?"

Gee sighed and glanced over at me, "Not for awhile, Pagan. He's got to deal with the voodoo creep stalking you."

I reached up and pulled the mirror down to study my eyes. Their normal color was back and the sickness in my stomach eased some.

"Your eyes were freaky Peggy Ann. I ain't gonna lie to you. That was some freaky, freaky shit."

"I know! Don't you think you should tell Dank?" I just wanted him back. I missed him and after my run-in with Leif I needed to feel secure. As much as I loved Gee she didn't give me the security I needed.

"I'll tell him but right now I'm not leaving you. The Voodoo prince is hot on your tail. So I need to stick close. No more running off to try and talk some sense into Dankmar."

I fought the urge to cry. Instead, I bit the inside of my cheek and kept my eyes focused on the passing houses.

"It's okay Peggy Ann. I got this."

I wasn't so sure about that but I sat silently as she sang off key to a Three Doors Down song that was playing on the radio.

Once we pulled into my driveway I didn't wait around for her to get out. If I couldn't have Dank then I wanted my mom. Thankfully, her car was here. As I reached the door I glanced back at Gee.

"I'm going to go hang out with my mom for awhile. You can make yourself at home in my room."

"While you're at it why don't you ask her about the Voodoo crap she's got you all mixed up in?" Gee replied, then vanished.

I walked inside and was relieved to see Mom curled up on the couch with a bowl of popcorn instead of tucked away in her office writing. CSI Miami I could drag her away from. Her writing, not so much.

"Hey sweetheart, did you enjoy eating over at Miranda's?"

I sank down beside her and grabbed a handful of popcorn wondering if I'd be able to actually eat it after the scare I'd just had. I needed to be careful how I sounded. If Mom heard even the slightest unease in my voice she'd perk up and begin grilling me with questions until I caved and told her everything. Focusing on keeping my tone casual and unaffected I replied, "Yep, we had boiled shrimp, corn on the cob and salad. The salad had raspberries, pecans, and goat cheese in it. It was surprisingly good. Even with the sweet dressing."

"Oh, that sounds yummy. I might have to call and get that recipe."

"You'll love it. Right up your alley in the healthy weird foods category."

Mom chuckled and nibbled on the handful of popcorn in her hand. I wasn't sure how to bring this up. Did I just say, "Hey Mom, remember when I was dying and you took me to that Voodoo doctor?" I had a feeling she would balk if I approached it directly like that. But it had to be true.

I turned my attention to the television and watched the crime scene of a strangled girl as the CSI crew did their thing. I popped one kernel into my mouth and managed to chew it up. The butter felt heavy on my sensitive stomach so I decided I better not try anymore.

"What's bothering you Pagan?"

I glanced over at Mom and she was studying me instead of the television. Figures she would pick up on my mood. The woman was impossible to hide a problem from.

"Um... I was just thinking about..." I paused and debated if I should even say anything. Did I really want to know this? I took in my mom's puckered eyebrows as she frowned at me waiting on me to finish. Her dark hair was tucked behind her ears and she was free of any makeup. I could see her concern and love glowing in her eyes. I knew why she'd done it. But I still needed to hear her explain. Maybe something she knew would help Dank end this. "You remember when I was sick as a kid," I began and watched as her frown deepened and she gave me a short nod.

"Well, I was dying. I remember that. And well... I had this dream. More like a memory. I was in an old shack and you were there too. There was this old lady." I stopped as the panic began to flicker in her eyes. It was true. I didn't need to explain anymore. She knew exactly what I had dreamed.

"It was real, wasn't it? You took me to a Voodoo doctor and she... or he healed me."

Mom swallowed hard and shook her head almost frantically, "Oh, god," she murmured looking down at her hand that had dropped the popcorn it had been holding. Had she really never expected me to remember?

"What did you promise them, Mom? What was their payment for healing me?"

Mom set the bowl on the coffee table in front of us and stood up. I sat there calmer than I actually felt as she began to pace back and forth in front of the television.

"Ohgod ohgod ohgod," she chanted under her breath. Now I was beginning to panic. This wasn't the reaction I'd expected. My cool, calm, collected mother had never had a breakdown on me.

"Tell me, Mom," I demanded.

She ran both her hands through her short hair and then rested them on her pajama clad hips. The flying pink pigs on her flannel bottoms were so happy and carefree and so incredibly out of place on the woman wearing them. I began to wonder if she was going to have some sort of panic attack the way her breathing had quickened.

"I didn't know what else to do," she whispered in a broken sob and wrapped her arms around her waist as if she needed to hold herself together.

"I understand that. What I need to know is what was the payment they required?"

Mom finally focused her grief stricken eyes on me, "Why're you asking me this? Has someone... has something... contacted you?"

Explaining that my boyfriend was Death and that a soul transporter was hanging out in my room probably listening to my iPod and painting her toenails an outrageous color didn't exactly sound like the best of plans. So I decided to go with something she would believe. "I had a dream. I saw it all. I remembered everything. Even the moldy stale smell."

A small amount of relief came over her tense expression. She nodded and wiped her palms on the front of her pajama pants nervously. "Okay. A dream. That's okay," she was talking more to herself than to me. I waited.

Finally she turned her gaze back to mine. "I was desperate Pagan. A nurse in the hospital told me about the voodoo doctor back in the swamp. I knew nothing of Voodoo. We'd been sent to The Children's Hospital in New Orleans because they had a specialist there that came highly recommended. The culture there was so different. I didn't know what to believe. I ignored her at first," she paused and took a deep breath. "But then...but then they told me you weren't going to wake up. I panicked. I took you to the old woman. I didn't know anything about her or her methods. I thought maybe she had a miracle drug," she let out a hard laugh. "I mean, who believes in spells anyway. I wasn't expecting her to actually brew up something and then the boy walked in." She closed her eyes tightly. I watched the creases on her forehead deepen. It had been Leif. I knew that without a doubt now.

"The boy was so young. But his eyes... his eyes were terrifying. He began chanting and this dark mist fell over the room." She opened her eyes and stared at me. I could see the memory of it in her eyes. The experience haunted her. "And then we woke up back in the hospital room. It was as if we'd never left. You were sitting up in bed chatting with a nurse and smiling. The circles under your eyes were gone. You wanted macaroni and cheese and someone had run off to find you some. Doctors and nurses began to pour into our room. You were a miracle. They had no explanation but there was no sign of the disease in your body," she swallowed so hard I could see her throat constrict. "There wasn't even any sign that the disease had ever been there. You made the news. You were a medical marvel. Then one day everyone forgot about it and it was as if it had never happened."

This was all she knew. She hadn't promised them anything. She'd just said she'd give them whatever they wanted. She had no idea she'd given them my soul. I stood up on shaky legs and walked around the table and hugged her. Not because she deserved it but because even though she'd made a grave mistake she'd done it because she loved me.

CHAPTER SEVEN

"Hey, what's wrong?"

I sniffled and looked up at a young boy about my age. His hair was blond and he had friendly blue eyes. I shrugged and wiped my nose on my sleeve. I wanted to be alone and cry. I didn't want to explain things to some stranger.

"Nothin','" I mumbled and stared down at my dirty tennis shoes. I'd just got my pink sparkly tennis shoes last week but now after running through the woods in the mud they were all dirty. Didn't matter. Mom was upset. I'd scared her. I didn't mean to. I never meant to. I needed to learn not to say anything.

"Something is bothering you," the boy said and sank down on the porch step beside me. Who was this kid?

"Just stuff," I muttered fiddling with my dirty shoe string.

"I'm good at fixing things. I bet if you told me I could help," he replied.

Was he for real? I just wanted him to leave me alone. Shrugging, I figured the truth would probably send him running away. I lifted my head and stared at him.

"I saw my dead Grandma today. We went to her house because she had a heart attack and died. Everyone put on dresses and went to visit her in her casket at her house and eat food and stuff. I saw her lying there. She looked asleep but she wasn't

breathing. Then I went into the kitchen to find the coloring books she always left for me. And there she was. Smiling like she always did. I was so happy to see she'd woken up. I went to hug her and she was gone."

I stopped, waiting for the horrified look my mother had given me when I told her this same story to come over his face but it didn't. Maybe he didn't understand.

"So, I spun around and there she was again. Standing behind me. She looked sad and she shook her head at me. I was just so happy to see her alive I ran to tell Mom. But when I got back into the room where the casket was my grandma was still lying there like she was asleep. My mother was still crying."

I stopped again waiting for the boy to jump up and run away from me. But he sat there waiting for me to say more. I'd wanted someone to listen to me today. Instead my mom had told me to stop it and threatened to ground me if I said anymore about this. Then she'd sobbed so loudly I felt sick. I didn't want to make her sad. I'd only been trying to make her feel better.

"Go on," the boy said.

"Well, I told my mom to come with me. I pulled her into the kitchen and there was my grandma standing there like I'd left her. She looked sad again and shook her head at me. My mom didn't see her. Instead she stared down at me and asked me what this was about. I pointed to my grandma and still my

mother didn't see anything. She frowned and looked back down at me and said she needed to get back to the visitors. Then I told her about grandma being there and Mom froze. The look on her face wasn't a happy one. She looked... really, really scared."

I didn't finish. I knew the boy would run away from me now.

"So, you saw the soul of your grandma," he replied matter of factly.

I nodded, "I guess, if that is like her ghost. Because I think I saw her ghost."

"Yes, it's like her ghost."

I wiped at my eyes. The tears had stopped since the boy had shown up.

"It's okay to see souls. It's not a bad thing. But your mom will never understand it. No one will. If you want to keep from upsetting people you need to act like you don't see them. If you ignore them then they'll leave you alone. If you let them know you can see them then they'll follow you around," he explained.

Frowning, I studied him. He seemed to know a lot about this. Did he see dead people too?

"How'd you know she wasn't the first one I've seen?"

He shrugged, "I guess you've been seeing them for about two years now."

My mouth fell open. How'd he know that?

"Do you see ghosts too?"

He nodded and a crooked grin appeared on his face. He really didn't think I was crazy.

"Yep, I see them."

"Can I make myself stop seeing them?"

He frowned and shook his head. He must wish he couldn't see them too.

"So we're stuck like this?"

"I'm afraid so," he replied. "But look at it this way, it makes you special. You can see something no one else can. Think of it as a super power instead of a bad thing."

Not likely. I wanted to be able to fly or maybe go invisible but I wasn't interested in seeing dead people.

"Pagan! Pagan! PEGGY ANN!"

My eyes snapped open and Gee hovered over my face.

"You were not supposed to go to sleep while I went to check out things outside and around the house. But what happens? I'm gone for maybe five minutes and you're asleep and that creep job is in your head."

I stretched and sat up on the couch. I was losing sleep due to these dreams. I couldn't help it that the moment I sat down I dozed off. Yawning, I shot Gee an annoyed glare.

"I couldn't help it."

"Well, it would be nice if you at least tried."

"This time I'm glad I did. He let me remember something I wanted to remember. It was a memory I'm glad he gave back to me."

Gee frowned, "What would that be?"

"The day of my grandmother's wake. I saw her. I saw her soul. She was smiling at me because

80

she knew I could see her. My mother, of course, freaked out when I told her about it but I got to say goodbye in a way." Pausing I directed my gaze to Gee. "Please tell me she isn't a lost soul. Please tell me Dank just hadn't retrieved her soul yet."

Gee stopped chewing on her thumb nail and shook her head, "Your grandmother has gone on. Dank checked on most all of your relatives. The ones you were close to have moved on. I know for a fact your grandmother's soul will return soon."

I let out a sigh of relief and wrapped my arms around my waist. It was a nice memory. I'd loved my grandmother. Upsetting my mother that day hadn't been something I remembered fondly but I understood why it upset her now.

"It was Leif that taught me to ignore the souls."

Gee rolled her eyes, "Well, let's give him a medal of honor for that act of kindness. Since the reason you can even see souls is because of him."

She was right of course. Still, the Leif from my dreams was so similar to the boy I had known this past year. It was hard to forget that. Nothing about him felt dangerous.

"Now, I want some of that chocolate stuff your mom made and I want to watch some more of that show we watched yesterday. I'm exhausted from taking care of your ass. I need some down time."

It had been days since I'd seen Dank and Gee hadn't left my side once. I knew this wasn't her ideal job and I hated she was growing tired of it. I got up from the couch and headed for the kitchen, "You want soda or milk with your brownies?" I asked her.

"Milk. It makes those brownies taste better."

The excitement in her voice caused me to laugh. I cut both of us a large chunk of brownie and poured two tall glasses of milk. We could comfort eat and watch *Gossip Girl* while she cackled and made fun of everything they did. The crew from the Upper East Side amused Gee to no end.

Dank

I hadn't seen Pagan in three days. Stepping into her room, I watched her as she brushed her hair. The jeans she was wearing were a little too snug for my comfort. I didn't handle jealousy well. It would be safer if she wore something a little less sexy. My eyes traveled up from the tall black leather boots she wore to the extremely tight fitting jeans that cupped her ass like a glove. Then the bare skin at the small of her back flashed at me as she raised her arms to twist the long dark locks of her hair up into a wild mass of curls on the back of her head. She was gorgeous and she was mine.

I closed the door behind me and she spun around startled. A smile instantly lit up her face when her eyes seemed to drink me in. She ran toward me and threw herself in my arms so quickly that a regular guy would have dropped her. The jean encased legs of hers I'd been admiring were firmly wrapped around my waist and she was raining kisses all over my face.

Was it possible for my heart to swell when I didn't have one? I tightened my hold on her waist, " I missed you too," I whispered, catching her busy lips with mine. She didn't press for more but let me taste just enough before pulling back and gazing down at me.

"I'm so excited. I've missed you like crazy."

"It's going to be hard for me to concentrate on that stage tonight with you strutting around in jeans that showcase your incredibly beautiful body. You know that right?"

Giggling, she wiggled in my arms and grabbed my face with both her hands and kissed my nose and forehead.

I immediately took advantage of the situation and laid her down on the bed. Her eyes went big and round with surprise as I lowered myself over her and began kissing her neck and taking small little licks at her collar bone. This was the kind of kissing we could do safely.

The pleased sigh from Pagan made me a little crazy. I loved the sexy little sounds she made when we were together like this. "Mmmmm, kiss my mouth," she whispered.

I shook my head knowing a kiss would end this moment too soon. I wasn't ready to stop just yet. I'd been fantasizing about her unique scent and taste for days. Now that I had her under me, I was greedy. I needed enough to get me through tonight.

"AH," she gasped as I bit the tender flesh at the curve of her neck and shoulder. Smiling against her warm silky skin, I inhaled deeply.

Pagan lifted her hips pressing closer to me. Insane need ignited inside me and I knew I needed to put distance between us. When she rubbed and pressed against me so trustingly it always ended up being my undoing. I pushed up from the close contact of our bodies putting some much needed space between the warmth she seemed so willing to share with me, I groaned in frustration and denial.

Pagan sat up and crawled over to wrap her arms around my neck. Her soft lips kissed my temple. "Trust me, Dank Walker I will only have eyes for you. No one else even comes close."

With a teasing growl I turned my head and nipped at her ear. "Good to know. No need for some clueless guy to meet Death tonight when it isn't his time to go."

"Dank!"

I chuckled and shrugged, "I'd say I was kidding but I'm not."

Pagan shook her head in exasperation and reached for her jacket then stood up. "Let's go see my rocker boyfriend in action," she replied with a smirk.

Tonight was about having fun with Pagan. I wasn't going to let the issues surrounding us get in the way. Leif had kept me away from her enough. I needed to do a gig with the band and Pagan wanted to experience it so this worked out perfectly.

Pagan walked into the hallway then glanced back over her shoulder and smiled, "You coming or what?"

Pagan

Smoke curled up from the floor of the stage as strobe lights flashed and fans screamed. Dank pulled me up against him and kissed my lips, "You stay here. I'll be back and forth between breaks. I want to be able to see you while I'm singing."

I nodded excitedly and he pressed one last kiss to my forehead before running out onto the stage where the other members of Cold Soul were already in place and ready to go. The full intensity of the stage lights came on and Dank joined the drummer and bass player in a wild intense opening to a song I didn't recognize.

Dank sauntered up to the microphone as his fingers danced across the guitar strings. I had the urge to scream along with the crowded civic center. The tight charcoal grey t-shirt he wore highlighted every delicious ripple in his stomach. I was very thankful for the guitar that covered his impressive abs. I didn't necessarily like the idea of the girls screaming his name getting such an eyeful of his perfectly formed body but I was forcing myself to deal.

His head turned and his eyes locked with mine. A pleased gleam flashed in them then he winked at me. Of course he'd heard my worries. Not surprising that he liked the fact I was unhappy about other females looking at him. The wicked grin on his lips grew and his sexy little dimple flashed at me.

I blew him a kiss and he reached up with one hand and acted as if he was catching it then touched his lips with two of his fingers before turning back to the crowd.   Honestly, I was very close to having a swoon moment myself. Who would have thought Death could be so incredibly sweet?

Suddenly the screaming crowd quieted as if on cue and Dank opened his mouth to sing.

"Daylight fades away as I watch you.
Darkness claims the sky and I wish you knew
that nothing you can do can keep me from you.
But I stay out of sight and only whisper to you.
Words I can't say. Words you don't need to hear.
Words I can't keep from tangling my way.
Now, I can't stand alone.
Now, I am under your influence.
You've taken over me and Now, I can't ignore what I've been shown.
You've claimed me and I don't care who knows.
You've claimed me and I don't care if it shows.
I'm weakened and I'm strengthened in your arms.
You've claimed me and I need to feel you close."

My heart sped up as his eyes turned to me. I hadn't heard this song before and I had all his albums on my iPod. His tongue barely peeked out from his lips as he wet them then held my gaze and opened his mouth again.

"You stand wanting more than you could ever understand.
I stand helpless needing to give in to your every command.
Wanting to see you smile has consumed me and tied both my hands.
Nothing I offer could ever be worthy of your love.
It's a miracle that you saw me and never ran.
I will spend my whole life trying to be the man you think I am.

Now, I can't stand alone. Now, I am under your influence.
You've taken over me and Now, I can't ignore what I've been shown.
You've claimed me and I don't care who knows.
You've claimed me and I don't care if it shows.
I'm weakened and I'm strengthened in your arms.
You've claimed me and I need to feel you close."

His lips puckered slowly as if to kiss me before he turned his attention back to the crowd and continued to sing.

"You hold fire within your gaze.
It mesmerizes everyone you allow into your maze.
I know nothing of your thoughts
but I need to bask within the warmth of your rays.
Nothing you do could ever be wrong.
You're forever perfect in every way.

Now, I can't stand alone. Now, I am under your influence.
You've taken over me and Now, I can't ignore what I've been shown.
You've claimed me and I don't care who knows.
You've claimed me and I don't care if it shows.
I'm weakened and I'm strengthened in your arms.
You've claimed me and I need to feel you close."

As the song came to an end the crowd began screaming out his name. Pride welled up inside me to think this brilliant... being was mine.

"So you're Dank's new fling?" I looked back over my shoulder to find the source of the snarky voice. The girl had an annoyed smirk on her very attractive face. A head full of blond curls hung almost to her tiny waist which seemed unfair considering the size of her chest. The tight tank top she was wearing had those double D's of hers spilling out of the low cut neckline. If she told me she'd just walked off a photo shoot for Playboy I wouldn't have been surprised.

"He normally goes for um... well a more *noticeable* type. I'm shocked you're what's keeping him so busy."

Yep, I hadn't mistaken the snarkiness in her tone. The girl didn't like me. But what she was saying made no sense. I knew for a fact Dank didn't have "flings" and that I was the only relationship he'd ever been in. I wasn't sure how to respond to her obvious lack of knowledge about him so I turned my attention back to the stage and watched as he brought thousands of people into a frenzy of excitement.

"Too good to talk to me, are you? Well, we'll see about that. I've been around a lot longer than you and my daddy is the reason Cold Soul even got recognized by a label. Dank won't like it that you were rude to me."

Finally unable to bite my tongue any longer I turned my head to meet her glare with my own. "When you say something worth responding to then I'll gladly reply. But it's obvious you don't know Dank at all. If you did you'd realize how incredibly idiotic you sound." Her eyes lit up with fury and I wanted to laugh at her reaction. The girl could dish it out but she sure couldn't take it.

"I hope you enjoyed your ride, slut, because it's over. Dank won't put up with that shit from you. I'm too important to upset."

My blood began to boil and I took a step toward her, "Did you just call *me* a *slut*?" I hissed.

She looked entirely too pleased with my anger at first but then her amused grin vanished and a terrified expression lit up her face. She began backing away from me. I wanted to laugh out loud. She reminded me of one of those bullies from elementary school that was all talk. Once someone called them out they backed down. I felt a sense of power at being able to handle this situation myself. Instead of waiting on Dank to set the bitch straight I was doing it.

"Don't," the girl backed up against the wall and I kept my angry glare fixed on her loving her horrified expression. This was fun.

"Pagan, stop."

I froze at the sound of Dank's voice as he stepped in between the two of us. The sweat on his chest had soaked into his shirt and it clung even tighter to his skin. Then he turned and looked back at the other girl.

"What's going on?" I heard him ask. What? Why was he worried about her?

"She attacked me, I was just trying to talk to her and she just attacked me," the girl blubbered in tears. She was crying? Dang, she even sounded believable.

"I didn't touch her. She--"

"Not now, Pagan," Dank interrupted me and I stood there gaping at him and the girl he was apparently consoling. Had I just stepped into some alternate universe? None of this made sense.

"She... she hissed at me," the girl stuttered, pointing one of her long red nails in my direction. Well, maybe I had done that. But she'd called me a slut.

"She called--" I began and once again Dank cut me off.

"Wait, Pagan."

Confusion quickly turned to anger and I didn't wait until he finished talking to the girl and listening to her mouthful of lies. He should be asking ME if I was okay. Not her. I wasn't going to stand around and listen to this. And I sure as hell wasn't going to stand there and try to defend myself to him if he wasn't going to even give me a chance to talk. I stalked toward the back entrance expecting Dank to get a clue and follow me but once I opened the back door that we'd entered when we arrived he still hadn't come after me.

Hurt, furious, and confused I stared out into the night. I didn't have a car. Dank wasn't coming after me. And he'd just completely blown me off and left me to hang in there. Tears blurred my eyes and I started to wipe them away and decided to leave them alone. No one was here to see me cry.

"I'll take you home," Leif's voice startled me. Spinning around I found him leaning up against his truck watching me.

Not wanting him to see me cry, I wiped at the tears running down my face. I couldn't get in a truck with Leif. He was an evil spirit after my soul. The concerned frown on his face reminded me of the boy who'd come to the hospital to see me after my wreck. He'd been so worried he'd slept outside in the waiting room all night. My entire life Leif had been there when I needed someone. Nothing about him was ever scary. Never once did he let me down. I glanced back at the closed door wishing Dank would walk through it but nothing happened. Anger burned my throat and my heart ached.

"Sure, thanks Leif. I could use a ride."

Dank

Letting Pagan walk off hurt and upset had almost been impossible. But the more distance she put between herself and the soulless creature in front of me the better. The anger and pain rolling off of her had been so distracting. I needed to figure out what this thing was. I couldn't do that with Pagan distressed behind me. I'd wanted to wrap her up in my arms and reassure her but I couldn't give this thing a chance to get away.

"Who are you?" I growled, glaring down at the blonde.

She smirked and straightened up from her cowering stance once Pagan rounded the corner.

"No one you know Dankmar," she replied and ran a long red fingernail up my shirt, "but we could change that."

I slapped her hand away with enough force that she gasped in pain. Good. I wanted her to hurt. She'd been too close to Pagan. And my foolishly brave girl had been glaring her down like she could take on a demon from Hell with her bare hands.

"You're beneath me," I reminded her in a cold flat voice. "Now tell me why you were near my Pagan." I demanded.

She shrugged and crossed her arms over her chest, "I did what I was told to do. It's my job, Dankmar. You understand about doing your job, don't you?"

"Don't play games with me. I want answers now. I need to get to Pagan. I don't have time for this."

She giggled and icy fear gripped me.

"Too late," she said in a sing-song voice before she vanished.

Not wanting to believe the truth hammering in my head, I broke into a run down the hallway Pagan had run to only a few minutes ago. There was no sign of her. I threw open the back door and the parking lot was full of empty cars. Nothing. Closing my eyes I searched for her soul. And for the first time since I met her I was unable to hear it.

"NOOOOOOO!"

CHAPTER EIGHT

Pagan

My eyes were so heavy. I couldn't remember why. I fought to open them but nothing. Where was I? What had I done? Where was Dank? Why wouldn't my eyes open?

"Shhhh, it's okay Pagan. Don't get all worked up. I've got you."

Leif's voice. Why was Leif here?

"Leif?"

Abnormally warm fingers brushed hair from my face and I shivered as goosebumps covered my body. They weren't from pleasure.

"Yes, I'm here," he murmured and continued playing with my hair.

"Where am I? Why can't I open my eyes?" the panic in my voice was evident.

"You're with me for now. Where you belong. Where you've always belonged. You've been mine since the moment I chose you when we were both just children. And as for your eyes they'll open soon enough. Your human body had difficulty dealing with the travel and for that I'm sorry."

Nothing he said made any sense.

"I don't understand."

"Just rest. You'll feel better soon."

I used every ounce of strength in my body fighting endlessly to open my eyes. But nothing happened. Everything remained dark. Until, exhausted, I slipped away into the darkness.

Blinking slowly, I stared up at what appeared to be black chiffon. Studying it in confusion I realized it was draped over the bed I was laying in. Turning my head to take in my surroundings I noticed the room was illuminated by a faint orange glow. I pushed up on my elbows and wondered if this was real or if I was dreaming. Candles covered the room and flickered causing light to dance across the ceiling. The walls were made of stone yet the room was elaborately decorated with silver candelabras and a crystal chandelier. I had to be dreaming. Shaking my head to clear it, I swung my feet over the side of the bed noticing for the first time the black silk sheets I'd been sleeping on. Like the other parts of the room the massive iron bed frame looked out of place in a room with stone walls. Where was I supposed to be and how had I conjured this place up?

I sat there studying the small flames in front of me and focused on what I could remember: I'd been at Dank's concert, There had been a girl... a mean girl. A girl Dank had taken up for. Oh, I'd run and Leif had found me.

Gasping, I jumped up and spun around looking for a door. This wasn't a dream. I needed to get out of here. Something wasn't right. Leif had taken me away. Drugged me. Why did I have to be such a drama queen and run away? Before I could work myself into a complete tizzy, the stone wall to the left of the bed began to move and a hidden door swung open.

Leif walked into the room dressed in his usual jeans and polo shirt. He looked so normal. He looked like a high school quarterback. His blond hair was perfectly messy as if it had been styled to look untouched. The blue eyes I'd once trusted sparkled as they met mine. It was so hard to believe he was evil.

"You're awake," he appeared pleased by this as he closed the door behind him.

"Where are we?"

Leif held out his hands and grinned, "My place. You like it?"

I didn't break eye contact with him. This wasn't the answer I was looking for and he knew it.

"Why am I here Leif?"

He smirked and lifted one eyebrow. This wasn't an expression I was familiar with. Leif never appeared cocky.

"Because you belong to me."

Forcing the panic that was trying so hard to break through further down while I held my calm expression I took another step toward him.

"I don't belong to you, Leif. I'm not a possession. I'm a person. Please take me back home."

Leif let out a hard laugh that held no humor, "So that *Dankmar* can have what I created? I don't think so Pagan," he stopped and ran his hand through the messy locks of hair. It was a move I'd seen him do hundreds of times. Somehow seeing that small touch of humanity eased the fear gripping me.

"You see, he was bound to love you. You're different. He saw that. But what he failed to explain is that you're different because I made you different. Not him. Not fate. Me. Everything about you has been molded into my creation. You were chosen for me." He held out his hand, "it's okay, trust me. My touch would never harm you."

Shaking my head I retreated until the iron footboard of the bed touched my back.

"Have I ever hurt you, Pagan? Listen to your soul. It knows where it belongs. The fire flashing in your eyes right now is your soul reaching for me." He stopped in front of me and smiled down at me like he had a wonderful secret to share. He held out his hand to me, "give me your hand."

My eyes. He was the reason my eyes were glowing a freaky orange color and he wanted me to give him my hand? I don't think so. This was a problem.

"Please Leif, take me home. I just want to go home," I pleaded.

Frowning, Leif dropped his outstretched hand. "What must I do to make you trust me? You trust Death without question. Death, Pagan. He is Death. How can you trust a creation meant to take souls from earth and not trust me? I've never let you get hurt. I've never left you alone. But he shows up and you fall mindlessly under his spell. What did he do to deserve you? He didn't save your life. He would've taken your soul when you were a kid. Left your mother grieving the loss of her child and not thought of it again. It's what he does."

"But why did you save me?"

Leif gave me a small sad smile and tilted his head to the side studying me. "I'm not your darkest dream, Pagan. I may walk in the darkness but I saw a life worth saving and I chose it. My father chose it. He agreed you were meant for me. Now it's up to you to accept that the life you have always lived is coming to an end. It is past time. You were supposed to die that day on the road and when Death came I was to take your soul instead. You would've trusted me. Your soul and my spirit are one. But Death broke the rules," Leif growled and stalked over to one of the many candles lighting the room, "I'd become lax in my judgment. I knew Death was with you but I believed he was doing what he does when he takes a special interest in a soul, preparing you. Instead, the fool was falling in love with you."

I watched horrified as he held his hand over the flame causing it to grow until the tip was licking against his palm. His fist tightened over the flame then he turned back to me and opened his hand to reveal a ball of fire.

"I may not control Death but I do control the dead. Those who made less than intelligent choices on earth. They walk among the darkness under my father's command. Under my command. I need someone to fill the loneliness. You've been my companion for over fifteen years now even if you don't realize it. But your memories will slowly return. You'll see that you do, in fact, belong to me."

Dank was stronger than this. I chanted that reminder in my head to keep my heart from racing in my chest. He would find me. Even if I was in the pits of Hell. Glancing around I seriously doubted that was where we were. Nothing about this place reminded me of Hell. Well, except that I was stuck in here with a Voodoo spirit lord.

"You're just going to take me from earth? What about my mother? I can't just leave her." That was actually the least of my worries but he'd brought up my mother's grieving so I thought I'd throw it back in his face.

Leif frowned and closed the distance between us causing my body to go on high alert. I had to mentally force myself not to recoil from his closeness. I wasn't sure how he'd handle that. He was bound and determined my soul was his but it sure didn't want to have anything to do with him.

"I'll take you back soon. She won't even realize you were gone. I just needed a place where I could talk to you. To explain, without," he paused and a sour expression curled his lips, "that stupid transporter or Dankmar continuously botching my attempts."

So he was taking me home. I wasn't going to be stuck in this creepy cellar room forever. This was the best news I'd heard since he walked into the room. Breathing became easier.

"You were worried I would hold you prisoner? Come on Pagan, you know me better than that. When have I not made sure you were happy? When have I ever intentionally hurt you? Never," he finished reaching out to grab my hand and hold it in his. I wanted to jerk it away and run to the other side of the room but I didn't. Angering him wasn't the best idea. If he was planning on letting me go home I didn't want to change his mind by pissing him off.

"What is it you want to talk to me about?" I asked in a soft non-confrontational tone. It seemed to please him and his boyish grin appeared. That was the Leif I knew. Just seeing his smile eased my mind.

"That's better. Your heart has slowed down. I don't like having you scared. I never want you to fear me."

Too bad. I wasn't a fan of evil spirits so I would always fear him.

"Come for a walk with me, please. We can talk while I show you around," he said tugging gently on my arm. I wasn't really in the mood to take a tour of Hell but I also wanted to go home so I let him lead me to the stone door that matched the walls perfectly. I'd have never known it existed had he not used it.

The cool moist air didn't surprise me as much as my surroundings did. This wasn't Hell. Although it smelled very similar to what I'd expect if it were. The steam rising from the black asphalt street in front of me was from the wet night air cooling it down from what must have been an abnormally warm winter day, not the pits of Hell. The old and weathered French buildings lining the street were filled with bars, dance clubs, and of course voodoo shops. I might not be in Hell but this was the closest thing to it. A door to the bar directly across from us opened and a man came stumbling out cackling loudly as a larger man threw him out then firmly closed the door. The small boy tap dancing only inches from the drunk man didn't even flinch as the man cursed and laughed while walking directly at him. Where were that boy's parents? It had to be midnight. A woman ran up the street squealing with laughter then stopped and lifted her already tiny top until both her breast bounced free and bare for the man chasing her. She then turned and continued to run from him in stiletto heels with her chest completely in view for the world to see. The man finally caught up with her and swung her up in his arms burying his face somewhere I'd rather not see. Jerking my gaze off them and their revolting behavior I saw a horse drawn buggy making its way toward us. I'd never really seen one of these in real life. I wondered if that was why the streets smelled of manure and vomit.

"Come on Pagan, you've got your eyeful. Let's go for a ride," Leif pulled me toward the carriage as the horse stopped in front of us.

"We're going to ride?" I asked as he lifted me up into the back of the buggy.

"Yep," he responded grinning and took the seat across from me instead of beside me. I was thankful for the distance from him but I didn't like the fact that his eyes would be fixed on me.

"So, what do you think of Bourbon Street? Everything you'd ever imagined?"

I could honestly say I'd never thought of Bourbon Street at all. Not once in my life did I imagine anything about it. Now, I knew the exact location in Louisiana Leif had brought me. I turned my attention back to the streets as we passed by them. Lights broadcasting naked women flashed in windows and chalkboards claiming to have the best gumbo in town also filled the streets. Voodoo shops were endless and the small little dolls I'd always thought of when someone mentioned Voodoo littered the windows. That was all I'd ever known of Voodoo. A little doll you stuck needles into when you disliked someone. It was an amusing thought, nothing more. How off track I'd been.

"These shops, the Voodoo ones...," I began and Leif chuckled.

"Are owned by regular people sucking the tourists dry. Not one of them hold any power. I'd guess if a real voodoo spirit were to grace their doors they'd close up and leave town. The real voodoo isn't along these streets. It can only be found deep in the swamp by those chosen by the spirits to embody it."

Oh fabulous, the evil spirits were picky. Doesn't that just make it all better. I didn't roll my eyes but the grin on Leif's face said he knew I was attempting to be on my best behavior.

The old French buildings began to give way to cleaner, more elegant buildings. I wondered how much of New Orleans I was going to see before I was sent back home.

"This is the Garden District. It is a nicer area. The most well preserved southern mansions can be found right here."

As fascinating as that was I wasn't interested in New Orleans neighborhoods.

"What did you want to talk to me about Leif? Why am I here?"

Leif leaned forward and rested his elbows on his knees. I straightened in my bench seat in order to keep a safe distance from him. Thankfully he didn't seem to notice.

"I know you understand now what your mother did. You remember all the times I've come to you in your life. You know it was me that day in the old Voodoo queen's home that removed the sickness from your body. Yes, I did it and I require, my father requires, a restitution for it. All gris gris comes with payment. Not the monetary kind like the voodoo shop owners require. Real Voodoo requires something more. The more difficult the request, the more the payment will be.

I wanted you to live Pagan. I'd watched you from the moment you arrived in New Orleans. The nurse watching over you was the granddaughter of the voodoo queen. She brought me to see you the first day you arrived. I was fascinated with your spunk. My father was looking for my mate and I went to him with the request to have you. He said we must wait. That if it was meant to happen then fate would play into our hands. When the doctors said you would not see another day, your mother went to the nurse and she brought you to the old voodoo queen who summoned me."

He stopped and studied me a moment. I'd known most of this already, except of course, the connection with the nurse. After taking a deep breath, almost a sigh, Leif continued, "A life cannot be spared for free. The cost is a life for a life. I saved your life and in doing so bought your soul. It has been mine since the day you were healed. I've been near you ever since."

My mother had sold my soul to the devil. That was what he was telling me. Except it was hard to think of Leif as the devil. He looked so normal sitting there in front of me. If only he were a normal boy I could break up with and walk away from.

"None of this makes sense. Why did you become human? Why did you ignore me for years? Why did you pretend with me? Why do you want me? Why can't you just let me go?" The questions spilled out of my mouth. And Leif started to open his mouth again when an angry sneer took its place. That was new. That most definitely did not look like the Leif I knew. What had I said to set him off and, ohgod, don't let him morph into a horrid demon.

"He's here. How the hell did Dankmar get here so quickly?" he roared and the buggy came to a stop. I took in my surroundings as Leif stood up and jumped down from the buggy leaving me alone. The street lights were dim and the nice lit up mansions and busy streets we'd been on earlier were gone. This was downright creepy. A hand grabbed my arm and I jerked around and screamed but it instantly died as Dank pulled me up into his arms.

"It's okay," he assured me and I let out a choked sob of relief. He was here. I was going home. He ran his hand down my hair. "Shhhh, I got you. He's gone."

"Where? Are you sure?" I whispered against his chest.

"Yes, he bolted instead of facing me. He's out-ranked Pagan. I told you that."

Nodding into his chest I wrapped my arms around his waist and inhaled his scent. I didn't care that he'd hurt my feelings earlier. I'd over-reacted. I just wanted to leave this place.

"Let's go home," he whispered in my ear.

CHAPTER NINE

Dank

"You won't end this if you stay here huddled over her like some damn guard dog," Gee grumbled from the chair that sat in the corner of Pagan's bedroom.

I didn't even take the time to sneer at her. I couldn't take my eyes off Pagan as she lay sleeping in her bed. Safe. She was here with me and she was safe. The rage inside of me from having her snatched away right under my nose boiled. I'd been lax in my dealings with these spirits but no more. They'd messed with the wrong guy. The next soulless creature they sent near Pagan would be ended. I wouldn't wait around to see what its intentions were. I would just end its existence. I'd be starting with Kendra. She wouldn't be another missing person. Unlike the weak spirit lord I could make sure no one remembered her. I wouldn't have to wait until their souls all forgot she existed. It would be a clean excision. Kendra should have vanished when Leif did. It bothered me she was still around although she'd caused no stir since his departure. I'd watched her but she'd acted as if she were the flighty air-headed cheerleader she had always been. Not once had she approached Pagan or tried to flirt with me in order to upset her. At least she had more sense than the one who created her and knew to leave me and mine alone.

"You have that 'I'm going to kick someone's ass' snarl on your face, Dankmar. What are you planning?" Gee demanded.

I'd almost forgotten Gee's presence in the room. She'd been here when we returned worried about Pagan. That was one thing I could say about Gee. She was loyal to a fault, and Pagan had managed to snare Gee's loyalty. Now getting rid of her was the problem.

"Kendra needs to go. Soulless creatures have no place here and I don't want her near Pagan."

"Oh goody. I like that plan. The bitch should've gone back when Leif did. I've been watching her at school and she isn't causing a problem but the fact remains she's there. Leif left her there for a reason."

"Exactly." For once we agreed. But then when it came to Pagan's safety Gee was always on board. Pagan muttered in her sleep and rolled over onto her back. I watched in awe as her eyelashes fluttered against her high cheekbones. The plump bottom lip I adored was sticking out just a little as if she were pouting. Dark silky locks of her hair fanned out around her on the pillow. Everything about her was incredible.

"Puhlease stop looking like a love sick puppy. It's annoying as hell," Gee teased.

"So, I've gone from a guard dog to a love sick puppy. What is it with you and your canine descriptions?"

Gee laughed softly, "I don't know. Maybe I need a dog."

"Yeah, like that's gonna happen. A transporter with a dog as a pet. Where you going to board him while you're working? On cloud nine?"

"Well, aren't you a barrel of laughs? For your information I figure if they will let Death have a human I can at least have a dog."

I started to respond when Pagan's eyes blinked slowly and she opened them. I could see her pupils dilate as she tried to focus.

"Hey you," she rasped in a sleepy voice. It was time for Gee to leave.

"Go Gee. I'll call for you when I need you here," I demanded without bothering to glance back at her. I enjoyed watching Pagan wake up and I didn't want to miss a second of it.

"I can see I'm not wanted here," Gee's amused tone caused the corners of Pagan's lips to lift.

"I'll see you soon Gee," Pagan called out as Gee left the room.

"That's better," I sighed, sitting down beside Pagan and leaning back against the headboard. I reached over and pulled Pagan up to lay her head on my chest.

"Mmmmhmmmm," she agreed, still not fully awake. Leif had drained her energy by apporting her human body. It was dangerous to apport a human yet the idiot had done so. Pagan would be feeling its effects for days. I'd brought her home via a private jet and she'd slept the entire way.

"I can't seem to keep my eyes open but I want to."

I played with her hair wrapping the strands around my fingers. "That would be Leif's fault. He used a method of transportation not meant for humans. For that he'll pay."

"I'm sorry I left," Pagan's small apology caused me to stiffen. She had no reason to apologize. I'd been panicked and handled the situation wrong.

"No, I'm sorry I didn't explain to you that the blond was soulless. I shouldn't have disregarded your feelings. Seeing her so close to you sent a jolt of fear through me. I'd been on a mission to find out why she was there."

Pagan yawned then tilted her head back to peer up at me, "She was soulless?"

I nodded, "She distracted me and upset you all for the purpose of Leif getting you alone. I fell right into their trap." Admitting my failure left a bitter taste in my mouth. I'd failed her twice now.

"No, I fell into their trap. You were trying to protect me and I acted like a silly jealous girl and ran off," the sleepiness was gone from her voice now. She didn't like for me to take the blame for anything. If I didn't defuse her she'd stand up and start ranting about how wrong I was.

"You were jealous," I teased and her determined gaze morphed into a bashful smile.

"You know I was. The girl was calling me your newest fling and acting like you dated a different girl every week. I knew she didn't know you very well just by that comment alone but then she called me a slut and well, I snapped."

"She called you a *what*? I wonder if Leif knows about that. Since he seems to think you belong to him I wonder how he'd feel knowing his little evil sidekick called you such a vulgar name," I paused and took a deep breath. Raging while I held a very sleepy and exhausted Pagan in my arms wasn't a good idea.

"I should have disposed of her right then," I muttered angrily to myself.

"No, you shouldn't have. Besides I was just being a jealous girl. If I'd kept my cool none of this would have happened.

"Hmm, I like you jealous."

Giggling, she pinched my nipple through the thin cotton of my shirt and I burst out laughing. The sound was still so new to me. Before Pagan I don't think I'd ever laughed.

Pagan

"So what are you and your sexy rocker boyfriend planning for Valentine's Day?" Miranda asked coming up beside me as soon as I stepped out of my car. I'd forgotten about Valentine's Day but I doubted Death actually acknowledged that holiday. Besides Dank had left again this morning. Gee would be here soon. I'd left her eating the leftover waffles and strawberry topping Mom had put out for me on the kitchen table before she'd left bright and early for a writer's convention in Chicago. She'd be gone all week. The way things were going at the moment that was probably for the best. This way Gee could remain in human form and roam my house freely while we waited on Dank to find an answer to my problem.

At the thought of Leif, I glanced over to his parking place and stopped walking at the sight of his truck parked in his spot. Ohgod he was here. What did that mean? Everyone had forgotten him. Now he was back.

"I know you broke up with Leif but, dang, you don't have to glare at his truck like it's the worst thing ever. So he's back from his trip up north visiting his grandparents. You'll get used to being around him again. No big."

His grandparents? What? And she remembered him. My head started pounding. This was too much. Nothing made any sense.

"There's my girls," Gee's voice broke into my internal panic attack and I swung my horrified expression toward her. She understood. Her eyes flickered over to Leif's truck and then back to me. "Well, lookie lookie, the king has returned or should I say 'prince," she smirked at her own joke and squeezed my arm. "Won't today just be loads of fun?"

I started to shake my head and she squeezed my arm tighter.

"Smile and be nice Peggy Ann. That's all you need to do. I got this," she hissed and led me toward the doors of the school. Miranda silently followed behind us which in itself was a miracle. But then Gee always freaked her out anyway.

Gee didn't stop pulling me until we reached my locker. Miranda had said her goodbyes and gone to wrap herself around Wyatt as soon as we entered the hallway. I was thankful for her departure because I needed to talk to Gee alone.

"What am I going to do?" I whispered as I glanced around frantically for any sign of Leif.

"You're going to act like everything is fine. He's your ex; act like girls do around their exes," Gee blew a bubble with the gum in her mouth as if this weren't a big freaking deal.

"Gee. You are aware that he's after my *soul*," I snapped angrily.

She rolled her eyes, "You are aware that he ain't got nothin' on Dank."

"But Dank isn't here."

"I am Peggy Ann. Besides he's here because Dank disposed of his little helper. He has no one to report back to him."

Little helper? What? "Can you elaborate on that one please?"

Gee leaned against the locker beside me and pulled a string of gum out of her mouth as she rested one booted foot on the bottom locker. "Kendra was soulless, sweetheart. Now she's no more. Dank was on a rampage when he got you back from New Orleans. He isn't a fan of the French Quarter you know. All those old French buildings bug him to no end. But me, I like all the alcohol. Except then there are the naked women. That can get a little annoying."

Kendra was soulless. I rested my forehead on the cool metal in front of me while Gee continued to prattle on about New Orleans. Of course, Kendra was soulless. That made complete sense. If Leif was so enamored with me then he'd never really be in a relationship with someone else. Her taunts were all meant to feed me right into Leif's arms. And Dank, he'd pretended with her because he was protecting me from her. God, I was an idiot.

"So, she's gone..." I muttered mostly to myself.

Gee stopped talking about beignets and their gift to the world and sighed, obviously frustrated that her attempt to change the subject had failed.

"Yep, and Dank does his clean up. Not a soul will remember her. No pun intended."

"Gee?"

"Yeah."

"I need a coke and a candy bar. Lots of chocolate."

Gee laughed and shoved off from her perch against the lockers. "I'm on it. I'll meet you in class."

"Thank you."

I watched her as she headed down the hallway toward the teacher's lounge.

Leif's laughter rang down the halls and I turned to see him standing among the same group of boys that always surrounded him. He didn't glance my way and the cheerleaders hung on his every word. It was as if nothing had happened this year. This was very similar to the same scene I'd witnessed the first day of school. The day I'd met Dank sitting in the back of my homeroom. Smiling, I turned and headed for homeroom. Things might be all screwed up now but just thinking about how sexy Dank had been that day while I tried so very hard not to stare at his adorable little dimple made things better. I'd thought he was just another soul back then. One that could actually talk. So much had changed. The soul I was convinced was stalking me wasn't that at all. He'd been here to take my soul because I was meant to die. But something changed his mind. I liked knowing I'd affected him in a way no other human ever had. He'd broken all the laws of the universe for me. He'd let me live.

"Coke and Snickers," Gee announced as she placed the cold can in my hand and dropped the Snickers down the front of my shirt.

"Gee," I squealed in surprise and quickly caught the candy bar before it hit the floor and was trampled on by the herd of students rushing from homeroom to second period.

"Beggars can't be choosers Pay-gan. Deal," she chimed beside me.

"You can be such a brat," I snapped opening the Snickers and taking a bite.

"Yep, but you love me anyway."

I could only nod. My mouth was full and of course she was right. I did love her.

"Hey! Where'd you get that?" Miranda demanded as she ran up next to me.

I tilted my head over at Gee, who smirked. We both knew there was no way Miranda would ask Gee for anything.

"Oh," was Miranda's reply. Then she seemed to get over it quickly enough and whispered loudly, "You talked to Leif yet? And how weird is it that Leif comes back right after Kendra up and moves? It's like we're playing musical chairs around this place."

I couldn't help but tense up at the mention of Leif and Kendra's name. If Miranda thought this was weird she'd really be weirded out by the truth. Trying to wrap my brain around the fact Kendra was a soulless creature was just too much. I had Leif and his claim on my soul to deal with. I was going to have to put Kendra and her existence out of my head. Maybe I'd forget her like everyone else eventually would.

Gee softly cleared her throat. "Nope, but she's about to and we get a front row seat. Damn, I should've grabbed some popcorn while I was in the lounge."

Leif was coming directly at us with his crooked grin and easy swagger. "Hey Pagan, how are you?" he asked, stopping in front of me so I couldn't go any further. Even though I was flanked on each side by Miranda and Gee I wished fervently that Dank were here.

"Um, good thanks, and you?" I could feel the eyes of other students glued to us. This was what everyone had been waiting for. The teenage drama and angst that fueled our lives. If they only knew.

"I see you've made a new friend," his gaze shifted to Gee and the warning gleam in his eyes was obvious. Was he actually challenging her?

"Uh, yeah, I have."

"Ya know what they say, out with the old," Gee piped up raising her eyebrows and glaring directly at him, "and in with the new and improved."

Leif stiffened and I worried she'd pushed him too far. We were in the hall with a bunch of humans. Maybe it would be wise if we kept the evil spirit prince calm.

"A matter of opinion," his voice was clipped and cold. Knowing Gee she'd get amusement from that and make this worse.

"Um, okay well, it was good to see you again Leif and I'll, uh, see ya around," I reached for Gee's arm and held it firmly in mine tugging her with me as I stepped around Leif and walked as quickly as possible toward the girls' restroom. I could hear Miranda's heavy breathing as she ran behind us to keep up. Where was Wyatt when you needed him? Not that it would do much good. Miranda would pick gossip and drama over a make-out session with her boyfriend any day.

"Dang, Peggy Ann you're running like the demons of Hell are on your tail," Gee chuckled at her own joke. I didn't find her one bit funny.

"Please be nice," I shifted my focus off Gee and found Miranda watching us with a look of worry mixed with determination on her face. I realized she was prepared for Gee to lash out at me and she was mentally getting ready to come to my defense.

"I was being nice," Gee drawled and jerked her arm out of my grasp. "Jeez, Pagan get a grip. Eat your chocolate and drink your soda. I think your sugar is low and it's making you bitchy."

Sighing, I leaned against the wall beside the sink and took a drink of the coke in my hand. I needed to talk with Gee alone but the protective stance Miranda had taken said she wasn't going anywhere. So, instead I ate my candy bar and shot warning glares in Gee's direction.

"When, uh, is uh, Dank gonna be back?" Miranda's voice trembled. Gee seemed to find this entertaining.

"Not sure, he'll probably call tonight."

"You gonna tell him Leif is back?" she asked cautiously.

Of course I was as soon as I saw him. Better yet I could send Gee to tell him. I wasn't sure I could convince her to leave me with Leif so close now but I was going to try my hardest.

"Sure, but it isn't a big deal. Leif broke things off with me before he left. He's just friendly. You know that." I didn't even sound remotely believable.

Miranda frowned and walked over to the mirror and began fixing a few of her curls that she thought were out of place. "Hmmm, well ex-boyfriends can be a problem. Even nice ones like Leif."

She had no idea. "I think everything will be fine."

Gee found this funny and I glowered in her direction which only caused her to cackle louder.

Miranda glanced back over her shoulder and frowned at Gee but didn't say anything.

"Okay, I'm finished. My *blood sugar* should be fine now. Let's get to class. We're probably late."

CHAPTER TEN

Dank

The soul standing beside me watched anxiously as the little boy standing over the soul's former body cried loudly. I didn't like situations like this. I needed a transporter immediately. However, I wasn't going to leave until someone heard the boy's cries and came running to check on him.

"Wake up Grandpa, come on wake up," the boy chanted, shaking the empty body lying in the field. Dirty tears streamed down the kid's face. Although he wanted to believe his grandfather was only sleeping he knew the truth. The sobs wracking his body were an indicator he'd already accepted the fact his grandpa had passed on.

I peered over at the soul whose face was tense with frustration. He didn't like seeing the boy upset.

"He'll be alright. You've had several years with him to make an impression on his life," I told the soul and his eyes lifted to meet mine. Some peace drifted over him.

"Sorry I'm late, Dankmar," Kitely apologized as she appeared to the right of the soul.

I nodded but didn't say anymore. The transporter took the soul and left. But I waited. Leaving the boy out here alone with his dead grandfather wasn't something I was comfortable with. Not that he would come to harm. His soul wasn't marked to leave the earth. His life would be a long one. But leaving him to grieve alone was wrong. I watched him grab handfuls of the old man's shirt and burry his face into the fabric. His sobs were growing quieter now. Acceptance always came easier to the young.

"COLBY!" A shrill female voice called out and I lifted my eyes to see a young woman with short red hair come running over the hill. The fear was etched on her face, her large brown eyes bright with anxiety from the cries of her child. She was worried about her son and didn't realize yet her father was gone. I peered down at the boy once more as he lifted his head and called out to his mother. My work here was done. So I left them.

The house smelled of ammonia and vapor rub. It was a familiar smell. All the houses of the elderly I visited smelled the same. The old lady, tucked firmly into her bed under several homemade quilts that were a mixture of brightly colored patterns that I had no doubt she'd made herself, stared up at me through cloudy eyes. She'd lived a long one. This had been a good life for her. One hundred and five years on this earth was a gift very few were given. Only the best, most honored souls were given these lives.

"Well, it's about time you got here," she whispered in a weak voice.

I couldn't help but chuckle. She'd been waiting on me. The oldest one always were. They knew when it was time. These were the easiest souls to take.

"I'm here on time, *cher*, you're just an impatient one," I teased her with the endearment her husband had used when he'd been alive. I remembered him murmuring, "I'll see you in the hereafter my *cher*," to her before he left his body. She'd smiled through her tears. That had been almost fifty years ago.

"Ah, you heard him," she smiled and the wrinkles in her face crinkled even more.

"I did."

"Well, let's get on with it, shall we, I'm ready to see my man," she whispered and a series of coughs wracked her small frail body. I reached for her soft cold hand and she gave me one small squeeze before I drew her soul out.

*   *   *

Gee was sitting in the purple chair that had once been where I spent my nights as I walked into Pagan's room. Shifting my gaze to the bed I realized it was empty. I glared at Gee, "Where is she?"

"Snippy, snippy Dankmar. Do you have low blood sugar too?" she drawled. What the hell did she mean by low blood sugar?

"Where is she Gee?"

Gee sighed loudly and stretched her legs out in front of her. For once she wasn't wearing the tall black army boots she was so fond of. Her feet were bare and her toenails were a hideous shade of bright green.

"She's in the bathroom, jeez."

I turned to stalk out of the room when Gee stopped me, "Um, Dankmar, I don't think she'll appreciate you barging in on her while she showers."

She was right of course. I wasn't thinking. It had been almost twenty-four hours since I'd seen her and I was growing more and more frustrated by the minute. Leif was completely off my radar and I was still at a standstill on how to deal with him. I'd thought after I disposed of Kendra he'd show up but I'd gotten no response.

"You missed an awfully fun day," Gee's sing-song voice wasn't something that I found comfort in. It meant she was about to say something that was bound to piss me off.

"What did I miss?

"Well, let's see, I found out Pagan has low blood sugar and becomes a complete b--witch if she doesn't eat a candy bar during a stressful moment. And I found out that Miranda does, in fact, love gossip and, quite possibly, Pagan more than she loves the tall lanky boy she hangs all over," Gee paused and then grimaced when she heard my angry snarl. I wasn't in the mood for games. "Oh, and Leif has returned from visiting his grandparents up North. The entire school was abuzz with excitement."

He'd returned to school. My disposing of Kendra hadn't sent him to me; it had sent him back into Pagan's world. I hadn't expected that.

"Is Pagan okay?"

Gee stood up and threw an amused smile my way before heading for the door, "Yes, of course. I

124

was on her like, um... I believe that old woman last week we took after she'd burnt down her house cooking said 'like white on rice'," Gee laughed. "That was one funny old lady. I hope I get to transport her soul again the next time around." Then Gee left the room.

The pale pink dress hanging on the outside of Pagan's closet door caught my attention. The soft fabric appeared almost precious enough to touch Pagan's skin. I walked over to it and picked up the dainty hem and rubbed the silky texture between my fingers.

"Do you like it?" Pagan asked before wrapping her arms around my waist.

"I love it. When will you wear it?" I inquired turning around in her arms to gaze down at her and soak in her features.

"Well," she bit the inside of her lip nervously then glanced around me to look at her dress. "I saw it at the store and I just... liked it. I guess I need somewhere to wear it..." she trailed off staring up at me hopefully. Was she asking me to take her somewhere nice? Our last few weeks had been anything but fun for her. We'd been dealing with Leif and his crap. Other than the concert that ended horribly I hadn't taken her anywhere.

The door creaked and I lifted my eyes to see Gee stick her head back inside. "It's called Valentine's Day, you moron," she announced. "If you're going to date a human, Dankmar, you need to remember their holidays." Gee gave me an exasperated look before closing the door once more.

Valentine's Day. I'd forgotten about that holiday. Holidays usually meant more work for me. Depressed people tended to end things on special occasions and party goers drank too much and then got behind the wheels of vehicles. But Valentine's Day wasn't too bad as far as suicides and car wrecks were concerned.

"I'm sorry, Pagan. I'm not very good at this, apparently. Can you forgive me for not thinking about the fact I need to do more than just show up in your bedroom or go with you to school? I'm a piss poor boyfriend aren't I?"

"Ignore Gee. She just likes to give you a hard time. Honestly, I didn't buy this in hopes you'd take me somewhere for Valentine's Day. I just saw it and I remembered that you wanted me to wear pale pink once, for the Homecoming Dance. I thought I'd get it and maybe when we had time I could wear it somewhere with you."

I kissed the top of her head. Leif was interfering in our lives and I didn't like it. My mind was focused so much on him and Pagan's soul; I'd neglected her. "Valentine's we have a date and I definitely want you to wear that dress."

Pagan

Dank was gone again today. He'd stayed the night with me or at least he'd been there when I feel asleep. Last night he'd played my song. I'd missed hearing him sing it.

There had been more words added this time as if he'd perfected it. The desperate sound in his voice had made me glad I was lying in my bed watching him. I was pretty sure I'd have become a puddle on the floor if I'd tried to stand up. His dark hair had fallen into his eyes as he looked down at the guitar in his hands and strummed the beginning of the song. I'd recognized it immediately. The words drifted through my head all morning as I hummed the hauntingly sweet melody.

"You weren't meant for the ice. You weren't made for the pain.
The world that lives inside of me brought only shame.
You were meant for castles and living in the sun.
The cold running through me should have made you run.

Yet you stay holding onto me
Yet you stay reaching out a hand that I pushed away
Yet you stay when I know it's not right for you
Yet you stay
Yet you stay

I can't feel the warmth. I need to feel the ice.
I want to hold it all in until I can't feel the knife.
So I push you away and I scream out your name
I know I can't need you yet you give in anyway

Yet you stay holding onto me
Yet you stay reaching out a hand that I pushed away
Yet you stay when I know it's not right for you
Yet you stay
Yet you stay

I can't feel the warmth. I need to feel the ice.
I want to hold it all in until I can't feel the knife.
So I push you away and I scream out your name
And I know I can't need you yet you give in anyway

Yet you stay holding onto me
Yet you stay reaching out a hand that I pushed away
Yet you stay when I know it's not right for you
Yet you stay
Yet you stay

Oh, the dark will always be my cloak and you are the
threat to unveil my pain.
So leave, leave and erase my memories
I need to face the life that was meant for me.
Don't stay and ruin all my plans
You can't have my soul, oh, I'm not a man
The empty vessel I dwell in is not meant to feel the
heat you bring
So I push you away and I push you away
Yet you stay
Ooooooh
Yet you stay
Yet you stay
Yet you stay"

"What has you looking all dreamy standing over here all alone?" Miranda asked, startling me out of my thoughts by slapping a hand against the closed locker beside mine. I couldn't keep the grin off my face.

"Dank," I replied.

Miranda raised her eyebrows and fanned herself with one hand, "Girl, I don't blame you, that boy can wear a pair of jeans like nobody's business."

I laughed and shook my head. Miranda truly appreciated men. She loved Wyatt but that didn't stop her from checking out the rest of the male population.

"Speaking of hotness, here comes your last drool-worthy boyfriend," Miranda whispered.

Not what I wanted to hear or deal with right now. Peering over my shoulder I watched as Leif spoke to those who passed him until he'd managed to work his way to me. It was so easy to pretend he was normal. Closing my locker door I turned around to face him.

"Leif," I muttered. It was the best I could do.

He apparently found this response amusing because his grin only grew bigger. "Pagan, it's good to see you too."

Haha. Wasn't he a riot?

"What do you need?" I asked a little too brusquely because Miranda elbowed me hard.

"Well, I was wondering about the tutoring. I mean, now that I'm back I need to keep up my grade and you know I can't do it without your help."

Whatever. There was no way a voodoo spirit was dyslexic. Did he think I was an idiot?

"Ah, well, when you *left* I filled your spot. But I'm sure there are other tutors available if you feel you *really* need one." I'd tried my best to get my point across without Miranda picking up on anything.

"But you were so helpful. I doubt anyone else will be able to help me the way you did." He was enjoying this. The gleam in his eyes said he was thoroughly enjoying every minute. I wanted to push him away and head to class but that would only cause drama and attention I didn't want. So instead I pulled my book bag up higher on my shoulder and stepped around him without another word. I heard Miranda apologizing for my behavior which was just ridiculous but she didn't know that.

"What's wrong with you? I mean, I know he broke up with you but you have Dank now. Why hold a grudge?" Miranda asked after she caught up with me.

I opened my mouth to respond when the ringing of her cell phone interrupted me.
Miranda rummaged through her bag in a hurry to find it before a teacher heard it.

"You know you should turn that thing off at school. You're going to get it confiscated again," I chided her.

She pulled it out of her bag and flashed me an annoyed glance before answering.

"Hello."

"Why? What's going on at the field?"

Miranda grabbed my arm to stop me. Her face looked puzzled. "We need to go down to the field. Not sure why but that was Krissy Lots and she said I needed to get down to the football field immediately then she hung up. There were sirens in the background."

"Sirens?" My interest had just gone from curiosity to alarm.

"You two need to come with me, now," Gee appeared in front of me and I really hoped I just hadn't noticed her walking up. Appearing out of nowhere would freak people out.

"We have to go to the football field," I explained, as Miranda ignored her and pushed past the other students

"I know you do," Gee replied without one ounce of her normally snarky attitude. Instead, she sounded worried. That could only mean... ohgod.

I didn't stand there and wait for an explanation. Instead, I took off after Miranda and we reached the door leading down to the football field at the same time. We ran the entire way toward a field that was now swarming with people and two ambulances. There was only one person we both knew that went to the field every morning to run. Wyatt.

CHAPTER ELEVEN

I was numb. Standing there as paramedics worked tirelessly over Wyatt's unresponsive body I couldn't seem to move. Miranda's sobbing and begging for Wyatt to wake up seemed so far away. Nothing felt real. Almost as if I were having an out of body experience. Other than my grandmother, I'd never experienced losing someone I loved. Surely he wasn't going to die. Wouldn't Dank have warned me? Didn't he know these things beforehand?

As if he heard his name in my thoughts he appeared, standing like a beautiful dark angel, behind the paramedic that was bent over Wyatt and administering CPR. They were getting the defibrillator ready to shock his heart. Nothing else had worked.

Dank's eyes met mine and I could see the sorrow there in those blue depths. This couldn't mean what I thought it did. He'd just come to reassure me, hadn't he? Wyatt was too young to just drop dead. He was my friend. Not just any friend but one I'd had my whole life or as long as I could remember. We'd had hotdog eating contests and raced dirt bikes. Wyatt had been the one to teach me to ride a skateboard and I'd been the one to bait his hook with chicken liver when we went fishing. He hated the stuff. Made him queasy. He was a part of my life and I didn't want to let him go. Didn't Dank see that?

"Wyatt, please baby, please, open your eyes for me," Miranda sobbed brokenly as they placed the two paddles on his chest the same way I'd seen them do to people on *Grey's Anatomy*. Wyatt's chest rose and fell in a quick jerk as they all seemed to be hovering over him begging him to respond. But nothing. I watched them do it again and with the same results. Nothing was happening. Then I watched as Wyatt's soul lifted from his body and went directly to Dank. Wyatt never looked back as a transporter I'd never met stepped forward and in an instant they were gone. Wyatt was gone.

The horror of what I'd just witnessed felt like a knife in my chest. He'd taken Wyatt from me. How could he take someone from me so easily? Miranda crumpled to the ground as the paramedics stated the time of death as 8:02. I couldn't bring myself to see if Dank was still here watching as our world fell apart. Instead, I walked over to Miranda and joined her on the dewymorning grass. Wrapping my arms around her body I let myself give into the pain.

The paramedics on the scene believed it was a brain aneurysm but no one would know for sure until after the autopsy. Seeing Wyatt's body zipped up in a body bag had been the most bizarre moment in my life. Although I knew he wasn't in there any longer it was still an odd moment. I'd fought the urge to jump up and run over to them and demand they let him go. He wouldn't be able to breathe in that bag. He hated enclosed spaces. Once I'd shut him up in my closet and locked the door and by the time I let him out he'd gone into a full anxiety attack. Now they were zipping him up in a bag and soon he'd be underground. We'd see him lying in a casket then he'd be lost to us forever. No basketball scholarship. No NBA. Wyatt was gone.

Miranda hadn't spoken or eaten since her mother had shown up after getting a call from the school. Miranda and I hadn't moved from our huddle on the ground when her mother arrived. I'd managed to coax Miranda to get up and we'd both ridden in the back of her mother's Cadillac to her house. Now she lay curled up in a ball on her pink fluffy bed with the stuffed animal Wyatt had given her for Valentine's Day last year. It'd had a necklace around its neck with a small heart shaped diamond. He'd saved up for almost a year to buy it for her. For twelve months he'd stop me in the hall at least twice a week and whisper how much closer to his goal he was. I'd smile and shake my head because they really were sickeningly sweet.

"How long you plan on staying here?" Gee asked and I jumped, startled by her arrival. I hadn't expected her to show up here. Frowning, I glanced over at Miranda and I wondered if she was asleep. I knew the pill her mother had given her as soon as we arrived had been to help her sleep.

"She's sleeping but she can't see or hear me anyway. I'm incognito," Gee explained.

I didn't want to go home. I didn't want to leave her. And truthfully I didn't want to see Dank. I was confused and hurt and Death wasn't really who I wanted to see at the moment. Miranda's room was safer.

"I'm staying the night. I'm not leaving until she's better," I replied in a clipped tone. Part of me was angry with Gee too. This was their job after all. Had they not considered I'd like to know about Wyatt's death? Maybe I could have stopped it. If I'd known he had an aneurysm I could have done something.

"You're mad at him, aren't you," Gee said matter of factly.

I only nodded.

"This was bound to happen sooner or later. You can't love Death, Pagan, and not accept him. It's what he was created for. He's not just some sexy guy who can sing and play the guitar."

I knew this, of course, but right now I didn't want to talk about it. Not with her and not with him. "Just tell him I need time. I don't want him showing up here. I don't want to deal with talking it out with him right now. I need to grieve, alone."

Gee opened her mouth to argue but closed it when I glared at her coldly.

"Okay, fine. If that's how you feel."

"It is."

Dank

"To say that she is pissed would be putting it mildly," Gee said as she stepped into Miranda's backyard where I'd been waiting since she went in to talk to Pagan. I hadn't felt comfortable barging in on Pagan while she was in Miranda's room. So instead, I'd sent Gee.

"What did she say?" The icy cold fear that I'd damaged the feelings Pagan had for me had been eating me up inside since I'd taken Wyatt's soul. If I'd only paid attention to the agenda and noticed his name but I'd skimmed it. This was the first time I'd missed something like this. I always noticed souls that held significance. I couldn't figure out how I'd missed Wyatt's soul. His death had surprised me as much as it did everyone else. If I'd known I'd have prepared Pagan.

When I'd arrived at the football field to find Wyatt's body, I'd almost refused to take his soul. But as I stood there watching Pagan, I knew I couldn't. I'd been given one reprieve from breaking the rules. I wouldn't be given another. And I couldn't leave her. My selfish nature won out. Unable to look her in the eyes I'd reached down and drawn his soul from his lifeless body. I'd met this soul before. This had been his third lifetime. Miranda's soul was his mate. Her grieving would be deep because she'd lost a part of herself. I hated knowing I had anything to do with it.

"She's upset, Dank. Right now, the fact you're Death sheds a whole new light on her understanding of you. Before today she'd never really soaked in your purpose because you'd never taken anyone from her. Now, she knows. She's battling the fact that to most humans Death is something they hate, fear, cower from and she's in love with him."

Self-loathing seeped into my skin and I bowed my head. This was inevitable. Death wasn't something humans loved. Now, my Pagan had realized how difficult loving me really was. I'd ripped up her world today and left it in shreds and there was not one damn thing I could do about it.

"She loves you, Dankmar. I know she does. But this isn't going to be easy for her to deal with. It's a hard concept for me and I'm not human. Her human brain will have a hard time processing everything. Just give her time and space."

Space? How was I going to give her space? I could hardly stand to be parted from her for hours at a time. How did I stand back and wait?

"How?" I asked, lifting my head to stare at Gee. Hoping for once in my existence she had something wise to say.

"How? Well, hell, Dank do I look like the freaking Creator? I don't know. You just do."

"I just do," I repeated, gazing up at the window where I could feel Pagan's heart beating. She was safe up there. I'd have to let her come to terms with who I am. Hopefully it wouldn't take too much time.

"You'll stay here and watch out for her?" I needed some reassurance that while she put distance between the two of us she'd still have someone near her.

Gee rolled her eyes and placed a hand on her hip. "You know it. I'm worried about her too, Dank. I'm not going anywhere. Since you don't have Pagan's desire to have you beside her weighing you down why don't you go deal with some voodoo spirits and kick some ass."

That was the first thing on my agenda. "I intend to. After this, dealing with Leif is the last thing she needs. I've got to figure out how to get rid of him."

Letting out a relieved sigh, Gee nodded her head in agreement. "Yes, you do and this is the perfect time to do it."

CHAPTER TWELVE

Pagan

Funeral homes were typically places I stayed away from, because wandering souls tended to get stuck in them. Today however, I sat beside Miranda holding her hand firmly in both of mine. We were put in the family section by Wyatt's mom. She'd said the two of us were as close to him as any of his family. Considering we'd faced every year of our lives together since preschool I'd have to agree. The Halloween we'd dressed up as the Three Musketeers came to my mind and a small smile played on my lips. I hadn't felt like smiling the past two days. Miranda and I had grieved together. Just yesterday we'd spent hours talking about different things Wyatt had done to make us laugh over the years. It had been bittersweet to remember him. After awhile Miranda had gotten so worked up again her mother had given her another sleeping pill.

Then there was the fact that I missed Dank. It felt almost as if I was betraying Wyatt to miss Dank but it couldn't be helped. I loved him. But I wasn't ready to face him just yet. Maybe after we'd buried Wyatt and adjusted to life without him I'd be able to talk to Dank. To look him in the eyes and not scream out in fury. I'd had enough time to think about it and I knew there must be a reason Dank didn't tell me. But I just wasn't ready to hear that reason yet.

My attention drifted to Leif as he walked inside and hugged Wyatt's mother then shook Wyatt's dad's hand before taking a seat among the other students who'd come today. Which was just about everyone. He just walked among them like he was one of them. Like he cared about Wyatt's death. It made me angry to think of how disrespectful his presence felt. Wyatt had thought Leif was his friend. He'd trusted Leif. All along Wyatt had never been more than a tool for Leif. A way to get close to me. Shifting my attention away from Leif before I completely got myself worked up I scanned the room.

The funeral didn't start for another thirty minutes. By that time the place would be standing room only. My gaze drifted over everyone I recognized from school. Some I knew, others I didn't. It's odd how when one of us dies we all come together as one. Even if we don't know each other or if we hate each other we come together for that one day.

I searched for my mother. She'd flown back home as soon as she'd heard and would be leaving again tomorrow. I'd assured her I wouldn't be leaving Miranda's for a few days so there was no need for her to stay home and miss the last two days of the convention for me. She was sitting beside Miranda's mother and father. I was glad she was here. Seeing her gave me some much needed strength.

The doors opened and in stepped someone I hadn't expected to be here today. Jay Potts had been my boyfriend from ninth grade up until the end of school last year when he'd decided to go off to college and his parents moved away as well. We'd broken things off because long distance relationships never worked. Seeing Jay saunter down the aisle I felt tears well up in my eyes. The four of us, Miranda, Wyatt, Jay and I had been a group from freshman year until the end of our junior year. So many of my high school memories of Wyatt were ones Jay was also a part of. His dark brown eyes found mine and he gave me a sad smile.

"Jay's here," Miranda whispered as she lifted her head and watched as he spoke with Wyatt's parents.

"I know." It seemed fitting that he was here at the end. Wyatt would have loved to see him.

"I'm glad," Miranda replied through her sniffles.

"Me too. Just seems right," I agreed.

Miranda laid her head over on my shoulder and we sat there huddled together while the preacher spoke and then the casket was closed and carried to the gravesite already prepared for Wyatt.

"I can't watch them lower him into the ground," the anxiety in Miranda's voice mixed with the trembling in her body told me it probably was a good idea for this to be as far as she went. I led her over to the steps on the far side of the funeral home so that we couldn't see the gravesite.

"Let's just sit here until they're finished." I coaxed

"Okay," she agreed and sank down on the cold cement beside me.

"That was awful, Pagan."

"Yeah, it was."

"Do you think his soul was around long enough to see it?"

I knew it wasn't but I didn't think that was the answer she wanted to hear.

"I don't know. Maybe. I guess anything is possible."

She nodded and twisted the handkerchief in her hands. I stared out over the cemetery and noticed a few lost souls hovering over gravesites. Those were the ones who'd seen their own funeral. They'd not wanted to go. I was glad Wyatt hadn't put up a fight. It was easier knowing he was going to have another life soon.

"Why're you mad at Dank?"

Miranda's question surprised me. I didn't think she'd have noticed my separation from Dank the past two days. She'd spent most of her time crying and sleeping.

"I never said I was mad at Dank," I replied.

"But you are. You don't have to say it."

Sighing, I rested my chin in the palms of my hands and leaned forward pressing my elbows into my knees.

"Just a little relationship drama. Not something worth talking about right now."

Miranda nodded and reached over for my hand.

"I love you, Pagan," she declared in a raspy voice.

"I love you, too."

Dank

Pagan and Miranda sat hip to hip holding hands as they stared out over the cemetery in front of them. I stood off to the side hidden from Pagan's sight and watched them. I knew she wouldn't want me here today. The thought made it difficult to function. She ran her hand over Miranda's curls in a comforting gesture I'd seen mothers use with their children. As much as I wanted to talk to her, to explain, I knew right now this is what she needed to do. It helped her grieve to comfort Miranda. They'd both lost someone special in their lives. Wyatt may have been the soul that was connected to Miranda's so therefore her pain was more intense but Pagan's soul was a kindred to Wyatt's. This was Pagan's first life and Wyatt's soul attached itself to hers.

Miranda laid her head down in Pagan's lap and Pagan reached up and wiped a tear from her eyes. I wanted to do that for her. I wanted to comfort her the way she was comforting her friend. But I couldn't. This was so damn hard.

Movement out of the corner of my vision caught my attention and I turned to see a guy making his way toward the girls. He was tall with long blond hair pulled back in a ponytail. The dark suit he wore meant he'd been at the funeral but I didn't recognize this kid from their school. Pagan had noticed him and Miranda was now sitting up. Both girls stood up to greet him. I watched as he hugged Miranda tightly and she cried softly in his arms as he spoke to her. He was assuring her that Wyatt was out there watching over her. He even said, "We know he can't stay away from you long. He'll always be hovering around you protecting you."

Then Miranda stepped back and he turned his gaze to Pagan. The translucent glow that intertwined connecting souls to their soulmates slowly wrapped around Pagan and the boy. Frozen in place, I watched in horror as Pagan stepped into his arms and he held her tighter than he'd held Miranda. With more familiarity. She'd been in his arms before.   W h e n Pagan stepped back from their embrace he seemed reluctant to let go. My legs began to move. This was not happening. His soul could go find itself some other soul to connect with. Pagan was mine. I already had a freaking voodoo spirit claiming her; I didn't need a damn human soul doing the same thing.

Pagan's eyes lifted and met mine. Instantly, she stepped back putting distance between her and the boy. I knew the blue in my eyes had gone from the normal human color to the glowing orbs that manifested when I felt emotion. I couldn't control their glow when I couldn't control my fury.

The guy finally tore his gaze off of Pagan and turned his head to see what had caught her attention. A small frown appeared on his face until he noticed my eyes. Then the fear all humans felt when met with Death's gaze came over his face. That's right buddy, I'm Death, now move away from my girl. I didn't say a word. Instead, I walked up the steps passing the boy and stopped in front of Pagan.

She swallowed nervously as she stared up at me. Then her gaze shifted toward the boy watching us. "Um, Jay, this is Dank Walker, my boyfriend."

I wanted to fall on my knees and beg her forgiveness. Hearing her still claim me as hers sent relief pouring through my cold form. Reaching for her hand I squeezed it and her thumb gently caressed the side of my hand. That was all the reassurance I needed. The soul behind me, obviously the soul meant to be her mate here on earth, meant nothing as long as Pagan wanted me.

"Dank," she said peering up at me, "this is Jay Potts. He's a, uh, friend of mine. He graduated last year and moved away for college. He and Wyatt were very close."

Jay Potts hadn't just been her friend. He'd been her boyfriend from the time she was a freshman until he broke it off at the end of last year. I knew she was worried about upsetting me and I couldn't blame her since I'd stalked over here with glowing eyes and a snarl. I turned my head and glared back at him. It couldn't be helped, I'd never like this guy.

"It's nice to meet you, Jay," I managed to say in a calm even voice.

A small snicker came from Miranda and I felt Pagan's body ease some. This was amusing Miranda and right now Pagan would suffer through anything that would put a smile on her friend's face.

"Uh, yeah, you too," he studied me a minute. My eyes were no longer glowing so he was probably trying to decide if he'd imagined it. His human brain would convince him it had been the sun hitting me just right or some other concocted story in order for it to make sense. Then something lit up his eyes, "Wait, Dank Walker, aren't you the lead singer for Cold Soul?"

The excitement and awe in his voice caused Pagan to completely ease up and she moved a little closer to me. I didn't want to talk to this guy. I wanted to wrap my arms around her and beg her to listen. To forgive what I was. But she wanted this meeting to go well. I could read it in her emotions.

"Yes, I am," I replied but as much as I loved her I could not even force a smile his way.

"No way, oh man, wow," he began shuffling through his pocket and pulled out his wallet. An old ticket stub from one of Cold Soul's concerts and a pen were shoved in front of my face. "Could you sign this? I'm a big fan. My ATO brothers will never believe this. This will get me out of clean up for at least a week.

Before I could even begin to understand what he'd just said Pagan replied, "Oh, congrats, Jay. I didn't know you got into Alpha Tau Omega. That's awesome. I know that was your main goal when you got accepted at UT."

He was a Greek. I knew what that was. I'd been to more frat parties than I cared to recall due to drunken stupidity.

Jay beamed over at Pagan, "Yep, rush was hard but I suffered through." He was still standing there with his pen and concert ticket in my personal space.

Pagan squeezed my hand and then let go. She wanted me to do this. Okay fine. I'd do it for her but I'd do it my way.

I took the ticket and pen and wrote a short note to Jay then scrawled the signature I'd adopted when I started the group Cold Soul. Shoving it back at him I then reached for Pagan's hand again and brought it to my lips.

"I miss you," I whispered and tears welled up in her eyes. I kissed her hand then brought it back down and let it go. I had somewhere I needed to go. Nothing was going to interfere with us again. I was tired of waiting around for Leif to make a move. I was ending this today.

Stepping back from her I nodded my goodbye and left the three of them there. I didn't worry about leaving Jay with Pagan this time. I was sure he'd get the message when he read his ticket.

After all when a guy reads,

She's mine. That's your one and only warning.
Dank Walker

He knows if he isn't ready for a fight he can't win then he'd better back the fuck off.

CHAPTER THIRTEEN

Pagan

Today was Valentine's Day. And I knew there was no way I'd be able to leave Miranda to go on a date with Dank. Wyatt had planned a romantic evening and he'd been teasing her with little notes for weeks that left hints about what they would be doing. I walked into Miranda's bedroom and she'd taken all those notes off her mirror and had them on her bed in a circle around her. The bear he'd given her last year was sitting in her lap and the necklace he'd saved so long for was in her hand. She was rubbing the smooth diamond as she stared at the notes in front of her.

When I closed the door behind me her head shot up and a small smile touched her lips. "Hey, I didn't expect you here today of all days. Don't you have a date?'

I shook my head and walked over to sit on the corner of the bed careful not to move or sit on one of those small slips of paper that were now treasures. "No, today I'm here with you. Dank can wait. I think you need me more than he does right now."

Miranda's smile wobbled and she squeezed the bear in her lap tighter. "I've reread all these hints a million times and I can't figure it out. He'd been planning it for months. You'd think..." her voice broke and she took a deep breath, "you'd think I'd have managed to figure out the surprise by now. But

Wyatt was so good at keeping secrets. He didn't want me to figure it out. He wanted to surprise me."

She was right of course. Wyatt loved teasing her. He'd teased her even back when we were kids. I'd always been the one tagging along doing the dangerous fun things and Miranda had looked like a little doll all dressed in pink watching us disapprovingly. He'd been enamored with her back then. She was something he didn't understand but even as a kid he wanted to touch her. He treated her like a fairy princess. Something breakable and precious. I'd always rolled my eyes in disgust but remembering them that way made me smile.

"I'll be okay, Pagan. You've spent every day with me since, since," she broke off and touched the picture that sat to the right of her bed. It was Wyatt in his basketball uniform smiling brightly with his MVP trophy from last year's State championship game. "Go with Dank. Have fun. For me."

I couldn't have fun with Dank knowing my best friend was curled up on her bed with notes from her dead boyfriend surrounding her while she mourned all alone. I needed to get her out of this room. "I have a better idea. Dank is busy tonight. I've released him from our plans and he decided he'd catch the Atlanta concert Cold Soul is having tonight. Originally he'd told them he couldn't make it but now he's already headed that way." Okay so I was lying but she'd never know that. "So you and I are going to go bake chocolate chip cookies and then watch the entire first season of *The Vampire Diaries*." I wasn't a

Vampire Diaries fan but Miranda was addicted to the show. She had every season on DVD and iTunes. She could watch it whereever she was. Like I said she was addicted.

Miranda rested her chin on the bear's head and peered over at me through her long lashes that curled up perfectly without any help at all. "Okay. I can do that," she replied.

"Of course you can. Now get up and let's go raid your momma's pantry for chocolate chips. Maybe she has some of those peanut butter chips again. We could make peanut butter chip cookies too."

Miranda sat the bear down and laid the necklace lovingly on the table beside Wyatt's picture. Then she carefully gathered up each note scattered around her bed counting them so she didn't miss one and then laid then beside the necklace. Once she was finished she turned to me, "Let's go make some cookies. I haven't eaten in days."

Dank

The smell of mold and earth and evil met my nose as I stepped into the old wooden shack. The rotten exterior of the house made it hard for me to believe it hadn't caved in from something as simple as a rain storm. The walls inside weren't much better from what I could see. Shelves filled with jars of items meant for spells and ridiculous concoctions meant to heal bodies, inflict sickness, remove memories and countless other purposes covered most of the walls. The people brave enough to venture out into this part of the swamp and walk through this door were the ones most desperate for an answer. Most people who knew of the true power of voodoo stayed away. It wasn't an evil humans needed to dabble in. It could possess you, steal your soul if you allowed it.

The old woman I'd come to see was sitting by the small coal fire and covered in a crocheted blanket. The rickety old rocking chair stopped moving the moment I'd entered the room. She'd felt me. Even one who'd lived a life controlled by the unholy union of voodoo knew when Death was near. She expected me soon but it wasn't her time just yet. I'd be back for her eventually and her soul was bound for eternal Hell. That I was sure of. A voodoo doctor never got another lifetime. Once they sold their souls that was it. No going back. The tin cup in her hands was set down beside her on a small handmade table. I could see the trembling of her arms as she carefully placed her cup down.

"May, de goose pimples say dat you here. Ahm ret to face de cos' for my choices," the old lady's voice shook as she addressed me. I appeared in front of her leaning against the warm black coal furnace.

"Ah not hyah for you soul jest yet," I drawled in the dialect I knew the old woman would understand easily.

Frowning she stared up at me, the whites of her eyes standing out against the darkness of her skin. "Whut you tink ah'm crazy?"

Chuckling, I shook my head no. "You might as well git it in dat haid, ah'm not hyah for you jest yet. Ahm not gon leaf befo I get wat I came for."

"Wat dat be? Sho don want de gris gris. Dis me know."

I nodded, "No gris gris, dat ain't why ah'm hyah."

She shifted in her chair and tried without success to sit up straighter. Her back humped forward so badly that it made her attempt impossible.

"Den tell me whut you wan an be don wit it. Me non lak you een hyah."

No, I'm sure she didn't like me in her home. I was the ending to her life. The only life she'd get. But I wasn't here to appease an old woman's fear. I was here to find out what exactly she did to Pagan.

"Tell me bout de gris gris dat saved de life of dat pischouette,"

The old woman began shaking her head with a look of horror in her eyes. "No, cain do dat. De spirit dat save dat gurl, he's mean lak a warse."

"Me know Ghede saved her. Ah'm not askin you dat. Whut needs to be don to end de gris gris curse on her soul?"

Her gnarled hands wrestled nervously with the afghan in her lap. Ghede was the voodoo spirt lord of the dead, Leif's father. In her religion he was the end-all. Even though I stood before her she wouldn't face me for all eternity. I'd simply remove her soul. Ghede would lord over her while she faced her eternity.

"Arryting Ghede do cos. Dat momma knew whut she's doin when she axe me to save dat beb."

"Den tell me whut dar can be don to change it," I demanded, growing tired of her dodging my question.

With a deep sigh, the woman lifted her glassy eyes to meet mine, "a soul for a soul is whut it cos. Nothin less wilt do. Maybe cos more. Ghede want dat gurl."

Stepping back out of the crumbling house I took in a deep breath of air. Although it wasn't exactly fresh it was better than the... *dank* smell inside the voodoo doctor's home. With a smirk at the irony, I glanced back over my shoulder one more time before leaving to go convince Pagan that she needed to confront the one person I knew needed to understand the consequences of her choices. Before Ghede decided to start demanding attention.

CHAPTER FOURTEEN

Pagan

Miranda had fallen asleep after episode four. I couldn't say I wasn't relieved. If I had to sit through one more Stephan and Elena scene I was going to scream. The angst was just a little too much for me at the moment. I turned off the television and pulled out a blanket from the ones Miranda's mother kept rolled up under the entertainment center and spread it out over Miranda's sleeping form. We'd left a mess in the kitchen and although I was sure her mother would just be thrilled Miranda had made cookies and actually eaten a few I didn't want to leave the mess for her to clean up.

Picking up the large plate with the remaining cookies and our two remaining glasses of milk I made my way to the kitchen. Once I stepped inside the doorway I saw Leif sitting at the table with his elbows resting on the tabletop and his gaze fixed on me, I almost screamed and dropped everything in my hands. I managed to swallow the startled scream in my throat and keep from making an even bigger mess in the kitchen.

"What are you doing here?" I asked, trying to remain calm as I walked over to the sink and put the glasses in the soapy water then placed the plate of cookies on the bar.

"Waiting until she fell asleep so I could see you. It is Valentine's Day, you know. I've been waiting years to spend it with you and have you actually remember. This was supposed to be my year. You'd have been with me eternally by now if Death hadn't lost his head once he got a look at you."

I rested a hand on my hip and glared at him. I wasn't in the mood for this. Not now. Not this week especially. "Listen Leif, you know what I've been through this week. Can't you respect that and just back off?" I snapped.

A look of tenderness flashed in his eyes and he lowered his gaze to his hands still resting on the table in front of him. "I'm sorry for your loss, Pagan. But if Dankmar hadn't screwed with fate you'd have never experienced the pain of losing Wyatt. The two of you were to have been the tragedies that hit our small town this school year."

My mind instantly went to Miranda. She'd have lost us both. Ohgod, that would have completely devastated her. She'd have crumbled. But Dank had stopped that. He may not have been able to stop Wyatt's fate but he did change mine. I'd be here to help Miranda heal and she'd be okay. She'd make it.

"Well then, it's a good thing Dank decided I was worth saving. Miranda could have never handled losing both of us only months apart."

Leif sighed and leaned back in the chair letting his hands fall to his lap. "Do you always think about others first, Pagan?"

His question surprised me. Of course not. Only a selfless person thought of others first and I wasn't selfless. When I wanted something I went after it and screw whoever stood in my way. "I only put those I love first but so do most people."

Leif shook his head, "No, they don't. Most humans put themselves before even those they love the most. It's their nature."

This conversation was getting off track. I wanted Leif gone so I could clean this kitchen and go to bed. "Just say what you came to say and leave, please. I don't want to chat with you."

"I told you I wanted to spend Valentine's Day with you this year. I even brought gifts," he flashed his crooked smile and from thin air pulled a dozen black and red roses along with an actual voodoo doll with a silver necklace around its small neck. The pendant hanging from it was a ruby cut into the shape of a moon.

I lifted my eyes to stare at him unsure what to think of this *gift.* "You got me a voodoo doll and black roses?" I asked incredulously.

Leif chuckled and leaned back in his chair. "I thought it would make you laugh. The necklace is your actual gift. And the roses as well. I happen to like black roses. They remind me of home."

Backing up some until the entire bar was between me and those very odd scary gifts I watched him closely. I didn't want him coming anywhere near me with that necklace. I knew that voodoo was big into talismans and if that was a talisman I didn't want it anywhere near me. No spirit was going to possess me.

Leif's amused grin fell into a frown. "You don't think it's funny, do you?" The voodoo doll and black roses were instantly gone and only a dozen red and pink roses remained along with the necklace that terrified me.

"Um, no, it's the necklace I want you to get away from me," I explained not taking my eyes off it as it lay harmlessly in his hand.

"Necklace? You're scared of the necklace? Why?"

"Because I don't want to be possessed by an evil spirit," I spat, backing up some more. I wondered if I screamed for Gee if she'd hear me. But then I'd risk waking up Miranda and this was not something she needed to witness.

Understanding dawned on him and Leif once again laughed. This was not funny. Why did he have to seem so amused all the time?

"You think this necklace is a talisman?"

"Yep, I'm not stupid Leif. I hang with Death, ya know."

Leif sighed and placed the necklace on the table. "I would never hurt you. I've told you that but you refuse to believe me,"

I didn't take my eyes off him as he stood there spreading the necklace out like it was a precious piece which only convinced me more it was full of all kinds of evil. Once he had it displayed on the table to his liking he lifted his eyes to mine.

"You know Pagan, fear can turn to love."

I stared at the necklace lying on the table unsure what to do with it. Heck, I was even afraid to touch the roses he'd left behind. Would picking them up and throwing them outside be dangerous? Maybe I should leave them there and go find Gee, or better yet, Dank.

Walking over to the doorway I peered into the living room to see Miranda still sound asleep. Good. I had time to do something about these *gifts* that really didn't need to be in her house before she woke up.

Dank

Her voice stirred me the moment she called out my name. I was standing outside her house preparing myself for the confrontation I was about to have with her mother when her voice reached me.

She was standing outside Miranda's house on the back porch when I reached her. A surprised gasp escaped her and then she smiled letting out a breath she must have been holding. "Oh, that was fast. Thank God," she said in a rush and ran over to me and wrapped her arms around my neck.

So far this was good. I'd have been here much sooner tonight if I'd thought this was the kind of reception I would get. Pulling her tighter up against my chest I inhaled the smell of her shampoo and kissed her temple. "Mmmm, this is nice," I muttered against her head. She sighed in my arms and then pulled back enough to see my face.

"I'm afraid it all goes downhill from here," she explained.

Not what I wanted to hear. I was hoping the next move would be her asking me to kiss her and then maybe take her home so I could cuddle in bed with her.

"Leif was here," she began and I tensed tearing my complete focus off her to let my senses scan the area for spirits. But I felt nothing. Except a small icy cold somewhere close by. It wasn't strong enough to be an actual spirit but it wasn't good either. Holding Pagan closer to me I reached further for the unwanted presence and realized it was inside the house.

"Who's inside?" I asked placing Pagan behind me and heading to the backdoor.

"What? No, he's gone. Miranda's in there sleeping," Pagan hurried to keep up behind me but at the mention of Miranda being alone I closed the distance quicker than a human could possibly travel and opened the door to find the throbbing dark essence lying on the kitchen table in the shape of a moon. The red stone almost had a pulse the evil inside it was so strong. Red and pink roses lay beside it and I stared at the items trying to figure out what it was I was seeing.

"That's what I called you for," Pagan huffed out after finally making it inside.

"The necklace?" I asked

"Yes, Leif left it and I'm scared to touch it."

My eyes shifted back to the roses. Had Leif brought those too?

"It isn't a necklace. It holds part of a voodoo spirit. Not the entire being, just enough so when you are near that spirit you will feel an attachment to it."

I heard the hiss of her breath as Pagan inhaled. "I knew it was something like that," she muttered angrily. There was my girl and her spunk. The voodoo prince had pissed her off. If I wasn't so upset about those dang roses I'd laugh.

"Where did the roses come from?"

"Leif, why? Are they full of evil crap too?"

So Leif had brought her the roses. Wait. There was something I was supposed to remember about today. The heart shaped boxes of chocolate I'd seen everywhere today as I'd retrieved souls.

It was Valentine's Day.

And I'd forgotten.

Well, hell.

"No, they're just roses," I replied. I didn't point out that they were beautiful roses. The kind only magic can produce. They'd probably never die. They'd be eternally beautiful if she placed them in a vase in her room. And then I could remember what an incredibly lousy boyfriend I was every time I saw them. Why is it that a voodoo spirit is better at this than I am?

"I still don't want them. Can I burn them?"

My heart didn't feel as heavy at hearing her distaste. I snapped my fingers and the roses caught on fire.

"Dank! What are you doing? You'll burn down the house or at least the table," Pagan ran over to the sink and I glanced back to see her filling up a pitcher of water. Crazy girl didn't think I'd protect the table. I snapped my fingers for effect and the fire went out leaving nothing behind. Not even a small pile of ash.

The water turned off behind me and I heard Pagan let out a small laugh. "Guess I saw fire and didn't think things through."

"It was cute," I replied and she blushed adorably.

"What about the necklace?" she asked her gaze flickering to the evil stone on the table.

"I can get rid of it just as easily if you promise not to run to the faucet for a pitcher of water this time," I teased.

Pagan giggled and nodded, "I think I can refrain."

I didn't even bother snapping this time. Instead I stared at it while the flames erupted and within seconds nothing remained.

Once there was nothing left behind by Leif, I turned my complete attention to Pagan.

"I'm sorry I missed Valentine's Day."

She smiled up at me, "It's okay. I spent most of the day with Miranda. We ate cookies and watched *Vampire Diaries*."

Tucking a lock of her hair behind her ear I remembered I did have something for her. I'd been waiting for the perfect time to show her and I couldn't think of a better time than now. "Come outside with me, I have something for you," I whispered before bending down and pressing a chaste kiss to her lips.

"Okay," her voice was soft and wispy. I liked knowing I still affected her even after everything I'd put her through.

Holding her hand I led her outside and down the stairs of the back porch until we were in the flower garden located in the far corner of Miranda's yard. I nodded my head to one of the ornate stone benches that lined the garden and then reached behind my back grinning. The crisp smooth texture of the wrapping paper I'd selected filled my hands and I pulled it around watching as her eyes lit up at the sight of the iridescent pale blue package.

"Nice trick," she teased grinning up at me.

I knelt down in front of her and placed the box in her hands. "Yeah well, I'm good for a few entertaining side shows now and then."

Biting her bottom lip anxiously she reached for it. "I almost hate to hurt the paper. It's beautiful."

"I'll buy you a whole roll, Pagan. Just open it."

Nodding, she ripped open the side and the paper was forgotten as it fluttered to the ground. The white satin box sat in her lap as she slowly opened the lid. I wasn't sure if she'd remember exactly what it was but I thought I'd wait and see if she worked this out on her own.

Pagan lifted the small gold brooch from the box. The flicker of emotion across her face told me she was working through the memories attached to the brooch in her hand. I'd been holding onto it for over fifteen years. Reverently she touched the pink glass stones that decorated the heart shaped filigree.

"Grandma gave this to me. I was sick and in the hospital and she'd come to stay with Mom at the hotel nearby. They took turns staying with me. Then Grandma had to go home because her heart was bothering her and her doctor wanted her home under observation. The day she left she brought me this brooch. She'd cried so hard as she'd told me to hold it close to my heart always. So I'd always know she loved me.

Pagan lifted her awed gaze to meet mine. "Then when... when..." she trailed off shaking her head in frustration. The memory was there. I knew it was and I wanted her to recall it without my help. It was one I'd waited patiently for her to remember since she'd discovered exactly who I was.

Her expressive green eyes showcased so many different emotions. Finally, she opened her mouth and whispered, "ohmygod," and I knew she'd remembered.

"Then *you*, Dank, YOU came to talk to me. To tell me that I was going to die but I'd get another life. My body was sick. That when you came back I was to go where you sent me and I'd come back again. Ohmygod," Pagan stopped and took a deep breath. "I gave you this brooch. I told you that I wanted to take it with me. You said that could be arranged and you slipped it into your pocket...but--"

"But you never saw me again. Because your soul was erased off the charts. The only reason I remembered you was because of this brooch. I knew there had been a soul that had been spared. Sometimes that happens. It's rare but sometimes the Creator changes his mind. I thought that had happened to you. So, I held onto that brooch given to me by a little girl who wanted to take something from this life on to her next. I figured once your name appeared on the books again I'd make sure you got your brooch just like you requested. But your name appeared so much sooner than I expected. It intrigued me. I couldn't understand why the Creator would stop your death as a child to take it only a few years later on the brink of adulthood. So, I came to watch you. To see what about this soul was so unique. Why it had broken all the molds I'd grown accustomed to over my existence."

Pagan's hand covered her mouth as a small sob escaped. I hadn't meant to make her cry. I'd just wanted to give her something she'd once held very dear.

"Oh, Dank," she cried flinging herself into my arms. "I can't believe I didn't remember you."

She was crying because she'd forgotten she'd met Death as a child?

Holding her in my arms I was at a loss for words. How did I comfort her about something like this?

"This is the most precious perfect gift anyone has ever received. You gave me back a memory that I will cherish forever. You gave me something from my grandma I didn't know I had. And you kept it and it led you back to me. It gave me you."

I felt a wetness in my eyes and I blinked confused from the strange sensation. A small trickle of water ran down my cheek. I stared into the darkness as I held Pagan in my arms in amazement. Death had just shed a tear.

CHAPTER FIFTEEN

Pagan

The little yellow daisy I'd picked out of momma's bouquet from her boyfriend looked kind of pitiful without all its petals. I twirled the remaining stem between my fingers and scowled at it. Stupid flowers. Stupid candy. Stupid stuffed bunnies with stupid purple fur. Oh and stupid, stupid heart-shaped balloons. It was all just stupid. I flung the stem in my hand into the creek behind my house.

The damaged daisy floated for a moment as the fast stream washed it away until I saw it slowly sink to the shallow muddy floor. Serves it right for being stupid, I thought with a huff. Crossing my now empty arms I glared at the water as it ran by. I didn't have anything else to do. So I'd just stand here and count all the stupid things about today.

"Not having a good day?" a familiar voice asked from behind me. I spun around and saw a blond boy with friendly blue eyes smiling at me. He seemed like someone I should know but I couldn't figure out where I'd seen him before. Maybe he played on one of the other teams we'd played in baseball this year. It's hard to recognize people when they don't have on their baseball cap and uniform. Out there they all look the same. I started to respond until I noticed the fluffy white stuffed puppy dog in his hand. The stuffed animal even had a red heart full of chocolate candy in

its paws. Even he got a stupid Valentine's present. I decided I didn't want to talk to him and turned back around to glare out at the water. Maybe he'd realize I was rude and he'd go away.

"You have something against stuffed animals and chocolate?" he asked in an amused tone. I didn't think he was funny. Not one bit. Stupid boy with his stupid Valentine's present. From some stupid girl.

"Yeah, what if I do?," I replied in a sour tone.

"Well, just seems like that's a funny thing to have a problem with. I mean there are lots of things to dislike. Snakes, for example, or spiders." He shuddered making me roll my eyes.

"I can dislike what I want,can't I? It's a free country."

He cleared his throat and it sounded suspiciously like he was covering up a laugh. I had a good mind to slug him one and see if he thought that was funny. Cause I knew for a fact I could throw a right hook better than most boys on my street. Nope, he wouldn't be laughing at all after I decked him.

"I guess you can. I'm just curious as to why you have a hatred against those items. Most girls like them," the fact he no longer sounded amused but actually confused saved him from my fist.

"You wanna know why?" I asked, shifting my angry glare his way. "I'll tell you why." I frowned, swallowing the knot in my throat. I hated that this actually made me want to cry. Stupid tears were for sissies.

"I'm listening," the boy coaxed.

"Because that's all everybody talked about today. They all flashed their chocolate hearts around and teddy bears and even stupid bunny rabbits as they walked down the halls. Balloons were tied on their chairs with those dumb cheesy lines 'I love you' on them. I mean, really, we are nine, people. We don't love anybody yet. At least not THAT way. And to make matters worse, stupid butt Jeff gave Miranda, my best friend, a purple bunny with a big 'ol balloon attached and a big box of chocolate. And did she share one piece of her candy with me? NOPE! She didn't. Said it wouldn't be romantic to give away a piece of her Valentine's candy. Then when I asked to feel the soft fur on her rabbit she shook her head and cuddled it up against her like I had a disease I could pass on to it. How absurd is that? Huh? Ridiculous right. Then I come home and my mom even has a big bouquet of flowers and a heart shaped box sitting on the table from her boyfriend. I thought for sure I'd get a piece of candy then. BUT NO! The box was already empty. She'd eaten it all. Why keep a stupid empty box?"

I stopped my angry tirade long enough to peek over at the boy through my hair and see if he was looking at me like a whiny baby. But he had that dumb smile on his face again. I guess since he got chocolate today then he thought it was funny I didn't.

I turned around thinking I could either slug him or tell him off then go back inside. But he held the puppy dog whose fur looked actually softer than that of the purple bunny Miranda had gotten from Jeff *and the box of chocolates out toward me. Confused, I lifted my eyes from them to look at him.*

"This is for you. You can feel the fur all you want and eat every one of those chocolates all by yourself. I brought it to you... that is if you want it."

"Me? But, why me? You don't even know me," *I stammered, wanting desperately to reach out and take the gifts. I really wanted that chocolate.*

"It's Valentine's Day and well, I've been watching you a long time and you're the only person I want to be my Valentine."

My eyes opened and the gold on the brooch that lay on the table beside my bed glittered with the early morning streams of light. I remembered that Valentine's Day. I'd been so hurt that no one wanted me to be their valentine. All the girls at school had been given something from a boy. Even Wyatt had given Julie Thursby something. But I hadn't got a thing. Wyatt had said boys didn't see me as a girl because I could run faster than them and hit a ball farther than they could. But it had still upset me.

Leif had known and brought me something. I'd eaten every one of those chocolates before I went to bed that night. Miraculously they hadn't given me a tummy ache like my mom said they would when I confessed at dinner that I was stuffed from the chocolate. Memories like this one made it very difficult to fear Leif. He really had been good to me all my life. Maybe he didn't have all bad qualities. The fact remained he wanted to take my soul to hell. Maybe that wasn't the way he looked at it but that was the way I looked at it. And being near him when he wasn't in "human" form gave me the creeps. I hated the feeling that crept over me when he was near. The hairs on my arms and neck stood straight up and I instantly recoiled.

Thinking back to that Valentine's Day I remembered the puppy. It was in the attic somewhere in a box. I hadn't been willing to get rid of it when I'd discarded all my childhood toys. I never could remember where I'd gotten it but it always seemed special to me. Like I wasn't supposed to get rid of it. I'd actually had a hard time putting it in the attic. Now the idea that there was a gift from a voodoo spirit in my house was unsettling. I needed to get it out. Sure I'd slept with it for years but that was before. This is now. I wanted it gone.

Sitting up in bed I decided I might need to wait and see if Gee or Dank showed up today. told him I intended to come home last night because I honestly hadn't. He'd thought I was staying with Miranda again and he said he and Gee would take turns watching the house. I'd left half expecting Gee to pop up out of nowhere but she hadn't. Then I'd crawled in bed and fell asleep.

My bedroom door swung open and in stalked Gee, "so here's the thing. I'm hanging outside Miranda's house not paying attention to anything all night because I'm bored out of my freaking wits. Then I finally realize I don't feel you in there. So I do a quick check and guess what? No Pagan." She swung her gaze over my way as she dropped into the chair in the corner and crossed her legs.

"So, I come here to check on you and low and behold you're here. I wasted an entire night in Miranda's backyard when I could've been eating food in your kitchen and watching the bad ass Chuck Bass on the television screen." She smiled amused with herself. "I rhymed. Bad ass Chuck Bass."

Rolling my eyes I stood up and walked over to my closet to grab a sweater. If Gee was here then we could go get that stuffed puppy out of my attic.

"Where ya going? I just got here." Gee grumbled.

"We're going to the attic. I have a stuffed puppy up there given to me by Leif I need to get out."

"What?"

"Just come on Gee, I'll explain while we're looking for it."

Dank

"Dankmar, I need to speak with you." Dank stopped outside Pagan's house and turned to see Jasyln. The anxiety on her face was alarming. Transporters typically had no real problems. Gee was an exception because she'd befriended a human. Jasyln was a typical transporter. Her only purpose was to handle souls.

"What is it Jaslyn? I haven't got much time."

"I realize that sir, but you need to hear what I have to say or um... explain, actually," she glanced nervously back at the house. "It has to do with your um... the soul you, uh..."

"It has to do with Pagan, the girl I love," I finished for her. She hadn't been sure of the terminology since she'd never felt emotion.

"Yes, Pagan. You see..." the nervous twisting of her hands was beginning to annoy me.

"Spit it out, Jasyln. If this is about Pagan then I need to know now."

Nodding briskly like a disobedient child who'd just been scolded she stared down at the ground. "You see sir, the boy whose soul I transported. The one that Pagan knew. He, uh, he wasn't supposed to die. That was not his fate. I didn't get very far before his soul was taken from me--"

"*WHAT* do you mean he wasn't supposed to die? His body was no longer usable. I was *drawn there*. His soul was barely hanging on to the body awaiting my arrival. And do you mean to tell me you LOST his soul?" I couldn't help the roar that left my body. This was not making any sense. Had Jasyln gone crazy?

"Yes, I know sir, I was drawn there too. But something happened. Another power took him. The power had the right due to a... a restitution."

Ice filled my hollow shell as understanding dawned on me. The restitution had taken a soul for a soul. One that would strike close to Pagan's heart. "No," I snapped stalking away from the door I'd been going to enter only minutes before. This could not be happening. Wyatt could not have lost his soul to Ghede because of Pagan. She'd never be able to live with herself if she knew. Yet could I keep this from her? I needed to get Wyatt's soul back. He might not be able to return to this life but his soul belonged to the Creator. Wyatt had done no wrong. He'd never sold himself to Ghede.

"Dankmar, sir, that isn't all," Jaslyn's soft whisper raked over me like razors. This could not get any worse.

"What?" I hissed glaring back at her.

"The Creator. He wants to see you. Now."

CHAPTER SIXTEEN

Pagan

"I think I may expire from inhalation of dust," Gee grumbled as she shifted another box off the piles of cardboard boxes my mother had placed up here over the years.

"Oh, stop being dramatic. What's a little dust? You've been in burning buildings."

"Yeah, well, I have to go into those. It's my job. However, my job does not say I have to do manual labor in an attic with a human."

Laughing to myself, I opened the box she'd just gotten down from the rather dangerously tall stack my mother had made. I mean, I get that she was trying to preserve space in here but a stack of boxes that almost touched the ceiling wasn't exactly a smart move.

"Do you want me to look in this one?" Gee asked as she got the next box down.

"Yes, please."

"And it's a white stuffed puppy right?"

"Yep... well, maybe not exactly white anymore. It was well loved so the fur may be a little discolored now."

Gee grumbled to herself as she began rummaging through her box.

I shifted through the items I'd packed away only eight years ago because I'd been unable to haul them off to the local Goodwill. A small purse with sequined letters that said Las Vegas made me smile. My mother had taken me on a writer's convention with her there once. It had been one of the last times she'd taken me with her. I always got bored but on the Las Vegas trip I'd found a friend... I think. Shaking my head I pushed it aside and found a Backstreet Boys t-shirt I'd gotten for Christmas one year. God, I'd been such a dork. A shoebox greeted me next that I knew without looking held all the letters I'd written back and forth with Miranda during school. They were full of insightful things such as "Do you think Kyle likes me?" or "Did you see the way Ashley's butt looks in those jeans, she needs to go on a diet," or my favorite, "Do you think Mrs. Nordman has a new chin hair today?" Yep, that shoebox was priceless. Unfortunately there was no stuffed puppy dog. Frustrated, I closed the box up and shoved it to the side.

"Well that one was a bust--" I slammed my hand over my mouth to keep from hooting with laughter. Gee was posing in front of the tall mirror that had once been in my 'princess' bedroom. But that wasn't the funny part. Gee had found my dress up clothes I'd not wanted to part with back when I was ten but didn't want in my room anymore either. She'd put on my Tinkerbell dress with a pair of Snow White plastic heels that her foot didn't come anywhere near fitting into. On her head she was wearing the veil headpiece that had gone with my Jasmine costume.

"How do I look?" she asked twirling around faster than a human would be able to making the

Tinkerbell skirt float out in front of her. I'd always twirled in that dress too trying my hardest to get it to stand out so perfectly.

"Fabulous, you should so wear it for work," I chirped then let out a trill of giggles.

"Dank wouldn't know what to think If I showed up looking like I was ready for a trip to Disney World. He'd be afraid to send the soul with me."

I sank down on the box behind me unable to stop laughing at the ridiculous sight.

"You'd scare him... to *death*!" I began laughing harder at my own little pun.

Gee started to say something else when a woosh behind me turned my laughter into a small squeal.

"What the heck, Jaslyn? This isn't a party," Gee complained and I eased some realizing Gee knew the gorgeous pale redhead that had appeared in my attic. Her perfect translucent features were so similar to Gee's when she was in "transporter" mode that I quickly put two and two together.

"I'm sorry, Gee," she stopped and slowly took in Gee's wardrobe with a confused frown on her face.

"Quit gawking Jas and tell me why you're here," Gee snapped. The dress-up clothes disappeared from her body and she was once again dressed in her jeans, hoodie and boots.

"Oh, um, yes... well, uh Dankmar needs you."

Gee's attention shifted from the transporter to me. "What about Pagan?"

"Oh, uh, he didn't say. He just said he needed you."

The frown on Gee's face told me she wasn't so sure about this. But if Dank had sent for her then it must be important.

"I'll go spend the day with Miranda. We can look for the pu-- the thing later," I piped up.

Gee nodded at me, "Okay, well go on down now before I leave. You don't need to stay up here by yourself."

"Okay."

I headed for the stairs then glanced back at Gee to ask her to please let me know if something was wrong but she was whispering with Jaslyn in a pretty intense conversation so I left them alone. Gee wouldn't be gone long. Dank wouldn't let her be. Besides, Dank was fine. He was Death. No need to worry.

Dank

"What's going on Dankmar?" Gee demanded as she arrived with Jasyln at the graveyard outside the small funeral home in Pagan's town. I'd been surveying Wyatt's grave to see if there had been any traces of activity. His soul had not been left to roam the earth. The only other place it could be was with Ghede in the Vilokan. If so, it was completely off the radar. Finding him would be near impossible. No Deity or being created by the Creator had ever been to Vilokan. The island under the sea was for the Voodoo spirits and the souls they claimed while on earth.

"Wyatt. His soul wasn't meant to be taken. He was never on the books." It still sounded unbelievable when I said it. Even after speaking with the Creator. Choices had been made. With the power of restitution on Ghede's side this could grow worse.

"*What?*" Her incredulous tone didn't surprise me. I'd had the same reaction. This had never happened. And if I didn't find a way to stop it the Creator expected me to hand over Pagan or her mother to Ghede. Neither of those were an option.

"Ghede, he took Wyatt's soul as payment for the restitution. The Creator doesn't believe he's going to stop there. Wyatt was just to warn Pagan or warn me. It won't be enough to make up for taking Pagan from his grasp."

Gee sank down on the headstone behind her, "Oh, *shit*."

"I don't want to tell Pagan this yet. Not if we can fix this without her knowing. The implications of Wyatt's death would be too much for her to deal with. She'd sacrifice herself without question. I won't allow it. I will stop this."

Gee nodded in complete agreement. I knew I'd be able to count on her. Jaslyn on the other hand was ready to offer Pagan up on a silver platter. She didn't understand but still it made it hard to have her near me. I wanted to take my anger out on someone and her indifference was placing her in the way of my wrath.

"Where is Pagan now?" I asked, jerking my scowl from the cowering Jaslyn back to Gee.

"She's with Miranda," she assured me.

That was good. I needed Gee right now. We had to find a way to penetrate Vilokan. Hell would have been so much easier.

Pagan

A day of shopping wasn't easy to convince Miranda to agree to but she needed to get out. After forcing clothes on her body and shoving her into my car, we'd headed to the mall. Four hours later she was showing signs of life again. I was extremely grateful.

"I need a coffee," I announced as we stepped out of our third shoe store in an hour. I'd managed to find two pairs of shoes I couldn't live without. One was a pair of yellow backless sandals that had a little heel. The other were beige colored boots that would match perfectly with my beige leather jacket. Best part was they were on sale. Miranda, however, hadn't bought a thing. We were slowly getting there. She'd actually tried on some shoes in the last store. I'd forced her to but at least she'd put them on.

"Me too," Miranda responded, turning toward the Starbucks instead of going to the next wing of the mall where Wide Mouth, Wyatt's favorite coffee shop, was located. I understood, and honestly, I wasn't sure I could deal with going into Wide Mouth right now either.

"What ya want?" I asked reaching for my wallet.

"I don't know, just get me whatever you're ordering," she said with a wave of her hand and walked over to find a table.

I couldn't order her what I was getting. I always ordered a caramel latte with whipped cream and so did Wyatt. I moved out of the way so the people behind me could order and I studied the menu up on the board behind the counter. It had been years since I'd had anything other than a caramel latte. I wasn't even sure if I knew something else to order.

"I hear the hot chocolate is incredible," Leif whispered in my ear. I knew he was actually here instead of just talking in my ear from the warmth of his chest behind me. He was also in human form because my arms weren't covered in goose bumps.

"I'm a big girl. I prefer coffee," I snapped without looking back at him.

He laughed softly, "Yes I know. Caramel latte with whipped cream."

Tensing I glanced over to where Miranda was sitting. She was watching us with an amused yet sad look in her face. I knew seeing me with Leif reminded her of Wyatt. Yet another reason to stay the heck away from him. If he'd only take the hint and leave me alone. I would never agree to give him my soul. Screw the stupid restitution or whatever it was.

"Nope," I replied and stepped up to the counter to order and put space between the two of us.

The girl at the counter was ogling Leif and not paying me one iota of attention. She actually began twirling a strand of her brown hair around her finger and batting her eyelashes. If the foolish girl only knew. He wasn't Mr. All-American.

I cleared my throat to get her attention and when that didn't work I literally had to slap my palm down on the counter in front of her, "Hello, excuse me, but it's my turn."

She finally tore her intense 'come and get me' stare off Leif and glared at me. Great, now she was going to spit in my coffee.

"I know that. I was waiting on you to order," the girl's tone was snarly.

"Well, I didn't realize that. You seemed preoccupied."

Her cheeks reddened and I was ready for her to unleash some snappy retort when Leif coughed loudly. He sounded suspiciously like he was covering up a laugh.

"I believe we've gotten off on the wrong foot," Leif's voice had gone smooth and deep. Just as he'd intended the girl's expression went all dreamy. Females really were weak when it came to attractive males. "We just need to order, I need a tall hot chocolate and you need a..." he was staring down at me as if we were here together. I started to open my mouth to correct this assumption when I decided I'd better go with it if I didn't want the girl's saliva in my latte.

"Oh, um, two tall... uh.... two tall.... um..." I could feel the impatient annoyed glare from the girl but I didn't let that deter me. I was trying to find something on the menu I knew would be safe for us to order.

"She'd like two tall mocha lattes with whipped cream and chocolate sprinkled on the top, please," Leif informed the girl.

What the heck? I hadn't given him permission to order for me. Even if what he ordered sounded really good. He stepped around me and began paying the girl while flirting with her; I crossed my arms and waited until he was done.

When he turned around to smile at me I snarled.

"What? You couldn't decide. I helped you out. You love chocolate. You'll like the mocha latte."

"I don't recall asking for your help. I can order for myself just fine," I hissed.

Leif shrugged and reached for my arm to pull me over to the side so the people I hadn't noticed behind us could order. I went with him then jerked my arm away from him once we were out of the way.

"Why are you insistent on being so angry with me all the time?"

He did not just ask me that. I opened my mouth to tell him exactly how I felt about his claim on my soul when Miranda stood up and ran toward the door of the coffee shop out into the mall.

I pushed past Leif and took off after her.

She had turned left and was headed for the back entrance we'd come in. I picked up my pace and dodged people who were all stopping to watch as I chased Miranda. My first concern was Miranda had flipped her lid with all this trauma. My second concern was that a cop was going to arrest me for trying to harm her. And then there was the concern I would accidentally mow someone down in my pursuit.

Thankfully, she stopped at the doors leading out into the parking lot where I'd parked. Her shoulders were heaving as she held onto the handle trying to catch her breath. Both of my bags she'd been holding were at her feet.

"Miranda, what's wrong?" I asked breathlessly as I finally caught up with her.

Tears were streaming down her cheeks as she stared outside. Devastation was so deeply etched in her face I wondered if the pain would ever go away. The girl I'd known my whole life had changed that day on the football field while we watched Wyatt's lifeless body lay there unresponsively.

"I can't," she sobbed shaking her head, "I just can't."

I wrapped my arm around her shoulders and pulled her against my side. She crumpled beside me sobbing pitifully. I'd pushed her too far today. She hadn't been ready for this. Guilt ate at me. I should have made this a shorter outing. Started her out a little at a time. Me and my big ideas.

"Come on, let's go home," I urged opening the door and leading her outside toward the car.

"Can we..." Miranda hiccuped, "can we just go visit his grave? I need to do that."

I disagreed. She wasn't ready for that just yet. I wasn't ready for that. But I couldn't tell her no either. I opened the passenger side door and Miranda slid inside.

Maybe, we could go. If that was what she wanted to do then I'd be tough and go with her. But first, we were going to stop by her house. She was going to need a little dose of courage and her mother had an entire cabinet with the liquid courage she would need.

CHAPTER SEVENTEEN

Graveyards at night are by far creepier than graveyards during the day. I tried desperately to ignore the souls hovering over graves I assumed were theirs. But it was really hard not to jump every time we walked past a grave and a soul floated in front of us. I wanted to grab Miranda's arm and stop her so the soul could wander past but that would only confuse her and alert the soul s that I could see them. So, instead I closed my eyes tightly and tried to pretend we weren't walking through souls. Oh, how I hated Leif's father for this stupid curse.

"It's chilly out here," Miranda said breaking the silence. I glanced over at her as she took another sip of the bottle of wine in her hands. I'd found a dessert wine that I knew she'd be able to handle. Coming to a graveyard at night was not my idea of a good time but I sure hadn't wanted to get out here and have her completely break down on me or, God forbid, go running into the night the way she'd run at the mall. I wasn't up for an evening jaunt down a soul-thick path.

"Yep," I agreed, pulling my beige leather jacket together and buttoning it up.

"You want some? It'll warm you up," Miranda offered me the bottle of wine.

I glanced down at it in her hand. The pale color and fruity smell was tempting. I could use something to ease my discomfort. But I was driving so I shook my head, "No, I'm good."

Miranda waited one more second before pulling the wine back to her chest, "Okay, if you're sure. But it really does help."

I wasn't going to argue with her. I was sure it was helping her tons. Three weeks ago I couldn't have paid her to walk through a graveyard at night. Heck, I couldn't have paid her to pull in the parking lot of a graveyard at night. Having someone she loved buried here changed things.

"There it is," she whispered, finally stopping.

My gaze followed hers. Wyatt's grave was still fresh and covered in flowers. A few were starting to wilt but for the most part the flowers were all still as lovely as they had been at his funeral.

"Let's go sit on the bench," Miranda said almost reverently.

Wyatt's parents had placed a bench at the foot of his grave. I'd wondered about that when I'd seen it the day of the funeral. I thought maybe it would just be there for the funeral but when we'd left I'd glanced back and it was still there.

"There's the one I sent," Miranda's voice broke as we sat down and stared at the flower arrangements in front of us. The large round basketball that lay on the head of his grave was made of orange carnations and black angel's breath. Miranda had been hysterically insistent that the florist make an arrangement that looked like a basketball.

They'd come through for her. It was beautiful. Wyatt would have loved it.

"It turned out really good," I assured her.

"Yeah, it did. I wish he could see it."

I wasn't sure how to respond to that. I didn't want her to start talking about his soul hanging around and seeing it before it passed on. Lying wasn't my strong suit and I had a hard time agreeing with her when I knew better.

"Remember that time we brought Wyatt's four-wheeler down here from that path in the woods behind his house?" Miranda's voice had taken on an amused sound.

"Yes." We'd been chased by the cops for jumping graves on his four-wheeler. Both Wyatt and I had taken the blame and left Miranda out of it. Wyatt had always been protective of her even back then and, in all honesty, she'd begged us not to do it. We'd listened to her the whole way over here about how wrong this was and how the ghost of the people's graves we jumped would haunt us. I'd, of course, known she was wrong and it didn't bother me at all.

"My mom still has no idea that happened. I didn't even tell her about you two getting in trouble because I was afraid she'd refuse to let me hang out with delinquents."

I laughed and a small smile touched Miranda's mouth. It was so good to see those. They were very few and far between.

Miranda took another swig of the wine. Her sips had progressed to swigs. The glassy look in her eye told me it was having the desired effect. I felt a little guilty for getting the wine for her but she needed to be relaxed to face this. She was reminiscing. That was good. It was worth a bottle of wine and underage drinking.

"Whoa, not who I expected to see here," Leif said as he walked up beside us. Miranda let out a small, then a giggle followed after she realized it was Leif and not a zombie who'd joined us.

"And drinking?" Leif's eyes lifted from Miranda's bottle of wine to meet my glare.

"She wanted to come here. I figured she needed some courage to face it."

Leif nodded and a small frown puckered his forehead. I wondered if he felt sorry for her loss or if he even missed Wyatt at all.

"I can understand that," he replied.

Miranda scooted closer to me and patted the spot beside her. "Come sit," she ordered Leif.

I wanted to tell her he was the most dangerous thing out here but I kept my mouth shut. At least on the other side of Miranda I didn't have to see his face.

"Here, it's good," Miranda replied shoving the bottle toward Leif clumsily. Okay, so maybe she'd had enough to drink.

"Don't mind if I do," he replied and I could see him tilt the bottle up from the corner of my eye.

"Sorry I ran off today and we juslefyouthere." Miranda was starting to slur. Yep she'd had enough. I reached across her and took the bottle from Leif.

"You've reached your limit Miranda. Any more and you'll hate me tomorrow," I explained pulling the cork out of my pocket and stopping it up before setting it down by my feet.

"I was worried about you but I saw Pagan caught up with you," Leif replied patting her knee.

"Yesss. Don know whatid do withouther," Miranda slurred.

Leif leaned forward and I could feel his eyes on me. "She's pretty special," he agreed.

Miranda nodded then started to lay her head on my shoulder but missed and fell forward. Both Leif and I grabbed her before she could topple face first into the fresh dirt and flowers.

Giggling, Miranda swayed back and forth as we sat her back up. She'd had way more than enough. I doubted she'd remember much in the morning. Hopefully, she wouldn't wake up hugging the toilet.

"Okay, I believe it's time for us to go home," I said reaching down to grab the bottle of wine and then stand up. "Come on, you. Let's get you to bed."

"I'll help you get her to the car," Leif offered and I started to tell him no when Miranda fell forward on her knees and cackled with laughter.

"Yeah, okay thanks," I muttered. It would be really helpful if Gee hadn't disappeared completely on me today. But I was on my own and Leif was the only 'being' stalking me at the moment. Leif looked entirely too pleased with this turn of events and I had to squelch the urge to tell him I could do this on my own. Because I was more than positive we'd end up sleeping in the graveyard if it was up to me to get her to the car.

Leif reached down and picked her up under her arms. She swayed on her feet and Leif wrapped his arm around her waist. "Easy girl," he coached.

"Easygirl," Miranda mimicked laughing like he'd said the funniest thing she'd ever heard. Note to self, Miranda was a lightweight. In the future one glass of wine was her limit.

"Bye Wyatt loveyousomuch," Miranda called out as Leif led her down the pathway we'd followed from the parking lot to get here. Like me Leif could see the souls and he dodged them and let them drift past so I didn't have to walk through any on the way out of here.

"Loveyousomuch," Miranda began to chant forlornly. The sad drunk was starting to emerge. I hadn't thought about that possibility.

Leif opened the passenger side door and eased Miranda into the seat instead of letting her fall inside. Which I had to admit was very thoughtful. Especially for a voodoo spirit.

I walked around to the driver's side when I heard the passenger side door close and the rear door open. Snapping my head around I watched as Leif got into the backseat. No way was that happening.

I stopped and opened the rear door on my side and stuck my head in. "What do you think you're doing?" I hissed.

"I'm making sure you two get home safely," he replied with a polite smile on his face.

"Oh no, you're not. Get out!"

"Donbesomean   Pagan," Miranda chimed in from the front.

Rolling my eyes I let out an exasperated sigh. Fine, if he wanted to be prince charming he could. I wasn't dealing with him right now. I needed to get Miranda home before she passed out, or worse, threw up in the car.

"Whatever," I grumbled and slammed the door for extra effect.

I managed to crank the car and pull out onto the road without once glancing back or acknowledging Leif's presence. I intended to ignore him the entire way home. Maybe he'd get miffed and disappear. God knows Miranda wouldn't realize it. I shifted my eyes over to her and saw her eyelids getting heavy.

"Stay awake. I won't be able to get you inside if you're passed out. We don't want your Daddy coming out and finding you like this."

That perked her up. If her Dad found her drunk he'd be furious. Well, maybe. Her parents had been so worried about her he might understand. Or they might admit her to a mental house. She really didn't want to go to one of those.

"That's better, keep those eyes open," I rolled down her window. "The cold air should help and if you start to feel sick please lean out that window and puke."

Miranda giggled and laid her head back against the headrest letting the cold breeze blow her hair across her face.

"Whose idea was it to get her wasted?" Leif asked from the backseat.

I was going to stick with my plan to ignore him so I reached for the volume to turn up when Miranda drawled, "Paaagaaans, shesosmart."

Leif chuckled from the backseat. I had to agree with him. I was questioning my intelligence at the moment too.

"Canwedoit agaaain to..tomorrow?" Miranda asked.

I shook my head, "No. Trust me, the headache you're going to have in the morning will agree with me. That was a one-time deal."

Miranda made a "pfft" sound that caused spit to spray from her mouth.

I pulled into Miranda's driveway fully expecting Leif to just evaporate when he opened the car door like a human and then proceeded to get Miranda out of the car. Great, Prince Charming was going to continue with his polite behavior. I followed them to the door and Miranda's mother met us there.

I stepped forward and handed her the half empty bottle of wine.

"She wanted to go see Wyatt's grave tonight. I took this because I felt like she would need it. I'm sorry--"

Her mother held up her hand to stop me. "No, it's okay. I understand. That's not any worse than the pills I've been giving her." Her mother's tone was so defeated. I'd heard that tone before with my mother. I hoped they weren't going to do with Miranda what my mom had done with me.

"Just go on home tonight Pagan. Your mom's already called me looking for you. Her plane arrived an hour ago. I'll look after Miranda tonight."

I nodded and stepped back as Miranda went into her mother's arms and she closed the door.

"Looks like it's just you and me," Leif said, entirely too pleased.

CHAPTER EIGHTEEN

"No, it's just me and I'm going home," I replied turning around and heading for the car. I didn't give him the pleasure of even looking back. I opened my car door with a little more passion than was actually required and got inside. Reaching up for the keys I'd left in the ignition I fumbled around and couldn't find them. Frustrated, I turned on the overhead light and peered around the steering wheel to see my keys weren't there.

I checked both my pockets and started to lean down and feel around in the floorboard when the passenger side door opened and Leif slid in with my keys dangling from his fingers.

Grrrrrr... I reached out and snatched them easily from his two finger hold and then shoved them into the ignition. "What do you plan on doing Leif? Going inside and visiting with my mom? Hmmm... because more than likely Gee is going to be there shortly after I arrive and she's chomping at the bit to kick your ass."

Leif leaned back in the seat making himself comfortable. "No, Pagan I just think you and I need to talk."

"About what? The fact you want to take my soul off to some voodoo hereafter or the fact that you stalked me my entire life then took my memories away from me? I know! You want to talk about how you *lied* to me about everything from the very beginning and made me think you were this nice guy. Pick a topic because I'm all talked out with them all."

Leif let out a weary sigh and rubbed his palm over his blue jean covered knee almost nervously. Back when I thought he was *human* I'd thought that was a cute gesture. Now, I wasn't very fond of it. "You're angry with me. I get it. I even understand it. I always expected you to be once you knew--"

"Then why do it?"

"Because I picked you. It was your purpose. It is your purpose. Don't you get it? You'd have died Pagan. Died. Gone on. Gotten another life and completely lost the chance at this life. Because you were going to die. Death wasn't in love with you then. He was going to take you like he was supposed to. There was nothing anyone could do to stop him, except your mother. She could choose to hand you over to Ghede and she did. She may not have realized it but when she begged a voodoo doctor to save you with voodoo magic she gave you over to my father. So you lived. You didn't die. Death didn't take you. You got to grow up with your mother and have friendships with Miranda and even Wyatt. You got to LIVE. Those were years you wouldn't have gotten had I not chosen you. This life you have now would have ended that night in the New Orleans Children's Hospital."

Hearing it explained like that was hard. Swallowing against the sudden lump in my throat I started to turn down my road when Leif grabbed the wheel.

"No. We aren't done talking."

I tried to turn but the wheel wouldn't budge. The car stayed headed east toward the outskirts of town and the old East Gulf bridge.

"Okay, fine. You kept me alive. I got to live this life. I appreciate it but now I want to keep it and you don't care. You claim to want me and need me but you couldn't care less what I want. It's all very selfish with you. It's all about what Leif wants. You take no consideration as to what I want. You act as if I'm your possession and I should just be happy about it."

Leif didn't respond right away. I tried to turn the wheel again and couldn't. I suspected if I took my hands off the wheel the car would drive itself. The idea that Leif might not let me go home began to set in. My heart rate picked up and I tried hard to remain calm. If that wasn't his plan I sure didn't want to give him any ideas.

"I've tried to make this easy on you. I've tried to make this transition one you could accept. I've sheltered you from the truth. I wanted you to make this decision because you wanted it. Not because I was forcing it but we've run out of time. There is something you need to know," Leif pointed toward the side of the road right before the bridge, "pull over."

I wasn't sure if he was directing me or the car because I wasn't about to pull over but the car pulled over and came to a stop without my help.

"What is it I need to know?" I asked hitting the stupid steering wheel for betraying me.

"You aren't going to like this. I didn't want you to ever know. But when you refused to accept that your soul was the restitution for the life my father granted you, my father decided he'd take his restitution elsewhere."

What in the world did that mean? Did this mean he was paid in full and I could get away scot free now because if so there wasn't anything about that I didn't like.

"Pagan, look at me," Leif ordered and I turned my head to meet his steady gaze.

"Wyatt's death was only the beginning. Ghede will take more. Everyone close to you. He'll take them one at a time until you either cave in and agree to come with me or there is no one else left to take."

Numbness settled over me as I stared back at Leif. It was as if he'd just spoken in a different language. I'd understood what he said but the meaning behind it was almost impossible for me to accept. I wanted to push it back, shove it away. He couldn't possibly have said what I just heard. There was no way that this restitution on my soul could affect others. Just me. Not... not Wyatt. No, I'd been there. I'd seen Dank. Leif was lying.

Shaking my head almost violently I yelled, "NO! YOU are lying. You are a liar. I saw Dank. I saw him draw out Wyatt's soul. Dank would have never taken a soul for your father. He would have never--"

"Dank didn't know." Leif interrupted me. "Did he tell you about it beforehand? Did he prepare you for the death of your friend? No. He didn't. Because Wyatt's death wasn't that of fate. My father used his power over your unpaid restitution to kill the body Wyatt's soul inhabited. Dank was drawn there to retrieve the soul from the body because that's his job. He was as surprised as you were."

I had no response. Dank hadn't told me. He never prepared me for it. Could this just happen? Could this spirit lord of the dead just take souls because I didn't do his bidding?

"But... but you said my death and Wyatt's death were to be the tragedies this school year. That would mean Wyatt's death was fate."

"I lied to you. I wanted you to be angry at Dank. I could feel your pain and I knew you were staying away from him."

Lies. Leif only seemed to know how to live by lies. He wanted me with him so he'd lied every way he could to get what he wanted. And now, his father was going to kill innocent people I loved if I didn't give in. Who would be next? My mom? Miranda? I couldn't wait and find out. This would not happen again. Dank had said he was bigger than this. He could end this but it was too late now. Wyatt had already lost his life because of me. I couldn't sit back and wait for someone else to die. The pain and guilt would be worse than an eternity with Leif. I let go of the tight grip I had on the steering wheel and my shoulders sagged in defeat.

"Okay. I'll go with you."

Leif didn't respond right away. The car started and it pulled back out onto the road. I watched in a haze as it drove itself toward the bridge. Instantly, my head slammed back on the headrest from the speed of the car and I reached frantically for the steering wheel and began pumping the useless brakes.

"Leif! Help me!" I cried and the steering wheel made a sharp turn to the right as soon as we were on the middle of the bridge.

"I got you Pagan," Leif's voice was calm and even as the car broke through the railing and we went careening out over the ocean waters below us. There wasn't even time for me to scream before everything went dark.

Dank

Gee appeared in front of me stopping me from going any further on my pursuit of voodoo spirits in their main mecca of New Orleans. I knew they had a portal here somewhere that led to Vilokan, the voodoo spirit afterworld. Only three places in the world had a portal. Over time New Orleans had become the most popular portal for the spirits. The humans here welcomed and celebrated them. Even the Catholics began accepting them and integrating them into their religion here.

"We have a problem," Gee's words weren't laced with sarcasm or humor. She was serious. Which meant whatever the problem was, it involved Pagan.

Bracing myself I asked, "What?"

"I went to check on her like you said. There were cop cars at her home. Her mother is very close to an emotional breakdown, if she hasn't already suffered one, and there are rescue boats, helicopters, and ambulances swarming the East Gulf Bridge. Pagan's car was found a mile or so down the river. There are skid marks on the bridge and a car sized opening on the railing where her car crashed through."

"She's not drowned," I stated, knowing Pagan's body was not dead. I'd not been summoned.

"Of course she isn't. But they all think she has. She brought Miranda home last night and Miranda was drunk. Leif helped get her to the house according to Miranda's mother. They're now guessing that she was probably intoxicated too and of course Leif is also missing, again, and they think both of them were in the car when it drove off the bridge."

"Vilokan," I growled. Leif had taken her to Vilokan. It was known to be an island under the water. But only voodoo spirits could enter through the bottom of the sea. The portals were the only way for anyone else to get in.

"That's what I thought too but he couldn't take her if she refused to go."

He'd told her. Leif had told her about Wyatt and of course she went. She'd do anything to save those she loved. I'd seen her give herself up for me without question. My beautiful soul was once again sacrificing herself. Damn Ghede. He'd pay for this.

He'd pay for it with the extinction of Voodoo. His world would be sealed off from this world. I'd make him wish he'd never come near Pagan.

With a roar of fury, I shoved the lamp post beside me hard enough to send it flying forward toward the center of the busy street. Glass shattered and people ran screaming as car horns blared.

"Brilliant move, Hulk. Go and kill somebody that isn't meant to die today, why doncha? As if the Creator isn't pissed enough right now." Gee grumbled before shoving past me and stalking away angrily.

I hadn't killed anyone. The most I'd done was caused some damage to a few cars and the lamp post. The chaos I'd created hadn't been intentional but it would come in handy.

CHAPTER NINETEEN

Pagan

Black chiffon floated above my head as I opened my eyes. This was familiar. I'd done this before. Blinking several times until I could focus, I studied the delicate fabric draped over my head. It was lovely yet creepy. Candles on all different kinds of silver candle holders filled the furniture around the room. Flames filled the room with a soothing glow. I'd been here before. Trying hard to concentrate I sat up and took in my surroundings. Stone walls surrounded me giving the large room an even darker feel. A large crystal chandelier hung in the center of the room. The ceiling was high and made of stone just like the walls. Slowly, my mind began working and I remembered this was Leif's room. He'd brought me here before. I was in New Orleans. This was good. There was a hidden door somewhere along this wall that would put me out onto Bourbon Street. I'd get out there and call for Dank. He'd come get me; I'd be fine.

I stood up and froze as more memories began to flash in my mind. My car flying down the road. I'd been unable to control it. Leif had been controlling it. He'd turned the wheel and we'd crashed through the railing and then we'd... then we'd...

"You're up," Leif's voice broke my concentration and I spun around to see him entering through a hidden door. It was on the other side of the room. Not the same one I remembered. How many doors were in this room?

"We. You, ran us off a bridge. Over the ocean."

Leif's easy smile fell some and he nodded slowly. He looked regretful at least for driving us over into the Gulf of Mexico.

"Yes, I did. I'm sorry but that was the quickest way to get us here without my having to apport you. Last time it really exhausted you but I had to bring you here in your human form. Trying to extract your soul would be impossible considering Death would never do that to you so I had to bring you to Vilokan via the closest route."

"Vilokan? What's Vilokan? Aren't we in New Orleans? And driving me off into the ocean is the closest route to *where*?"

Leif chuckled and sat down on the edge of the bed. I wanted to be angry with him but something in the back of my head that I was supposed to remember didn't allow me to blame him. "I'm sorry. Vilokan is my home. It's the spirit world in the voodoo religion. It's located under the water. It's a beautiful island. I can't wait to show it to you."

Shaking my head, I walked over to the door that last time had lead straight onto Bourbon street. "I've been out that door. I know what's out there. We aren't underwater. We're in a building on Bourbon Street."

Leif stood up and walked over to the wall and pushed on it, "No door, see."

"But I've been out that door," I insisted.

"Yes, when I made a door there you went out of it. But unless I make a door there then there isn't one. You went through a special portal that only voodoo spirits can create. We have three. One in New Orleans, one in Haiti, and one in Togo in Africa. All of those locations have the largest populations of believers. Our spirits are called there and we have the portals to bring humans or souls from those cities into Vilokan."

"Are you keeping me here?" The realization that this time I might be stuck in this underwater island began to sink in.

Leif frowned at me then understanding seemed to dawn on his face. "You don't remember. I should have guessed the travel would have messed with your head a little. It'll all come back to you but I won't make you sit around and wait for that."

Standing up, Leif closed the space between us and I started to back up when he placed his hands on each side of my head. Warmth radiated though my skull and slowly images began flashing in my eyes. Then, as if a movie screen was set up behind my eyelids, I remembered everything. Every awful detail.

Stepping back out of his grasp I covered my face with both my hands. I was here. Forever. Wyatt was gone because of me. Miranda had lost both of us because of me.   And Dank, he'd never know what happened to me. Could he even find me down here?

"I'm sorry, I had to remind you. Last night you only had to deal with this knowledge for a few short minutes before we went under. In time you'll heal from this. I promise," Leif's soothing tone was so out of place with the words that were coming out of his mouth. Did he even realize he'd just told me that I'd get over the fact my friend was DEAD because of ME? There was no getting over that. There was no getting over the fact I was stuck here for eternity with him while the guy I loved walked the Earth searching for me. My mother would mourn me. Miranda... ohgod I didn't want to think about Miranda. She wasn't emotionally stable. This wasn't something she was going to handle easily.

"I know it's a lot to take in right now. But all those things are of that world. You have to let go of the life you knew." Leif flashed a bright smile and spread his arms out wide as if offering me the world, "Pagan you can live here as you have never lived before."

I had no response for that. He truly didn't understand. The humanity I'd always thought he possessed, even in small amounts, really had all been an illusion. Leif's emotions and thoughts weren't that of a normal human. He believed he was offering me this wonderful world that was far greater than the world he'd taken me from. But I was a prisoner. I'd always be a prisoner. I was here because I couldn't allow his father to take any more souls. It was my soul that had been damned. It was my soul that would pay.

"Come with me. Let me show you the island. It's beautiful here. You'll love it. It's like no other paradise you could have imagined. We'll walk along the whitest shoreline and the water is a crystal clear blue. Then there is my father. He wants to officially meet you. And--"

"I'm not leaving this room." He may have the power to force me to stay here but that didn't mean I had to appease him. I wasn't a freaking pet he could play with. I was staying right here. Maybe I'd lose my mind and start talking to imaginary friends. That would be much more preferable than reality.

"Pagan, please don't be this way. You'll grow so bored in here. I want to show you all the things there are to love about Vilokan. It's your home now. Please, come with me."

No way in hell. I shook my head and walked over to sit down on the bed. "Do you have any books here? I'm doubting my iPhone works," I reached into my pocket to see if my phone was where I'd last stuck it. But, of course, it was gone.

"We have an entire library. Full of anything you could possibly want to read. Come with me. We'll get you so many you can't carry them all." The hope in his voice only ignited my fury more.

Shaking my head I snarled, "No thanks. I'll just sleep," I informed him, laying down on the black satin sheets, I turned my back to him. I wasn't going to be able to go to sleep but maybe if he thought I was

I'd be able to get rid of him for the time being. Having him here wasn't helping me cope with things. The door behind me opened and closed and I let out a sigh. Rolling onto my back, I stared up at the black chiffon and tried to imagine my eternity. It looked very bleak. Hopefully, insanity would claim me quickly.

I must have drifted off to sleep because the sound of the stone door moving startled me awake. Rubbing my eyes, I sat up and watched as Leif walked into the room.

His smile was tentative when his eyes met mine. Good, I'd made him nervous to approach me. Maybe I'd be the worst "companion" ever and he'd let me go and find a new playmate.

"You feel any better after your nap?" he asked, stopping at the foot of the bed.

No, I'd never feel better again. I didn't even give that question a response it was so ridiculous. Leif accepted my silence without much concern. He was dealing with my attitude entirely too well. And why was he wearing a tuxedo?

"Father would like for you to join us for dinner."

"No." Not ever.

"Pagan, you can't refuse Ghede. I can't protect you from any punishment he might decide you require. Please don't disobey him."

He has got to be kidding me. I'm stuck in the voodoo version of Hell and he thinks I care if I piss off his stupid daddy. "No," I repeated.

Leif's cool resolve began to crack a little. I could see the frustration in his eyes and I wondered if I actually could annoy him until he was begging to get rid of me. Of course he might not send me back to earth but throw me in their fiery pit or something. Did they even have one of those?

"Okay, listen. If you do this for me I'll... I'll send Wyatt's soul to you. You'll even be able to talk to him. His soul is different when it isn't on the earth. Once a soul without a body leaves the earth and dwells in the afterlife it can speak. It is only on earth that it requires a body for communication. However, when he speaks to you it will be different. He won't do so with his mouth. His voice will be in your head. His soul will speak to your soul."

Wyatt. I could see and talk to Wyatt. I stood up and walked around the bed toward the door. "Okay, let's do this."

Leif laughed from behind me, "I must make a note of this. I just have to find the correct incentive to get you up and moving. Wish I'd thought about Wyatt earlier. And you can't wear that to dinner. Ghede requires proper respect. You'll need to dress according to his wishes."

"Well, Ghede will have to get over it because when you drove me off the freaking bridge I only had a pair of jeans, a sweater and a leather jacket. I didn't exactly pack for this excursion."

Grinning, Leif gave a small hand gesture that looked more like a pathetic attempt at waving off a fly. "There, you look lovely and father will be pleased."

Glancing down I sucked in a breath. I had been unaware that I had any cleavage but the tight bust of the ridiculously extravagant dress had my boobs pushed up to my nose. Or so it seemed. The skirt of the dress stood out around me like a hoop. What was this the 1800s?

"Why did you just put me in a Scarlett O'Hara dress? You all are aware that we moved past this fashion more than a hundred years ago?"

Leif chuckled and offered me his elbow, "My father enjoys a party. Mardi Gras is his favorite time of year. Today Mardi Gras is in full swing along the streets of New Orleans so father holds his own celebrations down here. He'll likely throw beads at everyone at the table and serve us all King Cake. You'll like him, really. He is known for being the life of the party."

"Really? And here I thought he was known for being the wicked evil spirit of the dead. Silly me."

Leif shook his head at me, "You can't say things like that, Pagan. He won't approve. I can't keep him from punishing you. Please watch what you say. If you anger him I won't be able to bring Wyatt to you tonight."

That was enough to shut me up. I'd have to bite my tongue and deal with it. Glaring down at the lavender gown and dark purple beads that adorned it I wondered if I would have to endure these ridiculous dresses every night. If so, did that mean I'd get to see Wyatt?

"Come on. Dinner awaits and you've got to be hungry."

My stomach growled in reply and Leif grinned before opening the door and allowing me to step out. This time there were no smelly streets. Instead, the wide hallway was lit with gas lanterns and ornate carvings along the walls of masks. They were the sort of masks you see in pictures of costume balls. Fancy and well... exquisite were the only ways to describe them.

"These are all memories from Mardi Gras past. Each year father holds a costume ball on Fat Tuesday and every mask in attendance is forever remembered on these walls."

If I didn't despise everything about this place I might find that interesting.

CHAPTER TWENTY

Dank

Pagan's mother was grieving. I could hear her pain from outside the house. I'd been gone for two days looking for some way to penetrate Vilokan. But Pagan wouldn't want her mother to mourn her death. She wouldn't want to know her mother was having a complete emotional breakdown. Right now this was the only thing I could do for her and in return I could find out if there was anything her mother remembered about that night in the voodoo doctor's shack.

Knocking on the door would be what she expected. She saw me as Pagan's boyfriend. If I wanted her to believe I was not human I'd have to arrive a different way. I just hoped I didn't scare her too badly.

I appeared on the bar stool directly in front of Pagan's mother. She was sitting at the table with a cup of coffee. I could smell the whiskey in her drink. Sunken eyes that were highlighted with dark rings from no sleep lifted to meet my gaze. Surprisingly, she didn't even flinch. Instead, she stared directly at me and studied me silently. There were no tear streaks running down her face. Those had all been cried out. Her face was one of complete loss and heartbreak. I'd seen this expression on other mothers as they faced the loss of their child. But this mother's pain caused my chest to hurt. Maybe because I shared that pain.

Although I knew Pagan wasn't dead, she was gone. For now.

"Dank," she finally spoke. Her voice was raw and raspy from little use.

"Yes," I replied, waiting on her to say more.

She didn't right away. Her head tilted and she searched my face for the answers to the questions I knew were piling up in her head. She thought she'd drunk herself to sleep and was dreaming. Possibly hallucinating. Several different explanations ran through her foggy thoughts.

"How did you--?" She trailed off not sure exactly what to say. How did I just appear out of nowhere? I could still see the uncertainty in her eyes.

"Because I'm not a human. I'm something more." I let her soak in that information.

She took a weary sigh and pushed the cup of coffee and whiskey away from her, "Well, I've had too much of that I guess."

"I'm not a hallucination. I've been here in your house most nights since the moment Pagan's soul was marked for death. Watching her."

"You knew she was going to die?" Her mother's question was a mix of confusion and anger.

Shaking my head I held her gaze. "No. Pagan isn't dead. I didn't allow her to die in the car accident months ago that should have taken her life and she didn't die when her car went off that bridge."

Pushing herself back away from the table her mother stood up. "I need to go to bed. I'm not sleeping and now I'm losing my mind," she muttered.

I stood up and moved into her path stopping her. "No. You aren't. I'm real and I am telling you Pagan is alive. Her soul is still with her body. However, the voodoo spirit you sold it to when she was a child has a claim on it and right this very moment he has her. I need you to listen to me, believe me and help me."

Slowly her mother's face turned from one of disbelief to horror. Backing up until her legs met the leather chair behind her and she fell back into it, the understanding sank in. I wasn't sure if she believed it or not but she knew my words held some truth.

"Voodoo spirit?" she whispered brokenly.

"Yes, the one you opened Pagan's soul up to when you took her to the voodoo doctor in order to save her life."

She shook her head and lifted her eyes back to mine, "I never promised her soul. I'd never do something like that. I just asked that they perform whatever special magic or miracle potion to heal her. The nurse, the nurse said that her grandmother could help us. I was desperate and willing to try any other avenue. Traditional medicine wasn't working. I figured the herbs and natural remedies the old woman had might have some chance of doing something the doctors couldn't. I never... never... promised her *soul*."

Humans were so naïve to the supernatural powers around them. So many believed things all had an easy explanation. The concepts of magic and powers were so far-fetched that they assumed it was a natural cure. That a medical explanation would cover it all. "Voodoo isn't herbs and natural remedies. It's a religion. One that is made powerful by evil spirits when humans believe in them. If you don't believe then it can't harm you. But if you ever entrust it to answer your request you are in debt to the spirit that responds. You wanted to save your daughter's life. There is only one voodoo spirit that can do that. A powerful one. The spirit lord of the dead can grant life. He's fond of granting the lives of children. But not because he is malevolent. Because then he owns their soul. You asked the voodoo doctor to do whatever she could. She herself could do nothing. She's just a vessel used by the voodoo spirits. However, Ghede, the spirit lord of the dead, could do something. And he did. He gave Pagan life when it was her fate to pass on. Her soul was to have a short life this time. Her next life would have been longer. But this life was to end. You allowed evil to change that because you weren't willing to let her go. Now, Ghede has come to claim what is rightfully his."

She didn't speak right away. I watched as my words sunk in and she digested everything I'd told her. It wasn't easy for humans to understand. At least not the spiritual ones. But I hoped that because she had experienced the power of voodoo all those years ago she'd at least open her mind.

"You're telling me Pagan is with... she's in--"

"Vilokan, the afterlife or spiritual realm where the spirits of voodoo dwell. She's there in human form. They can't take her soul from her body without

Death and I can assure you Death will not take her soul." Explaining to her that I was Death would be pushing things a little too far. She'd taken in all her mind could handle.

"How do I...? What do I do? If she's in Vilokan is there a way I can ask for her back? What? How do I fix this?"

"You don't. But I will. I just need you to think about that night. From the moment the nurse came and got you to the moment Pagan was cured. Then I need you to remember Pagan's childhood. There was this boy, a blond boy, that came into her life several times. I need you to try very hard to remember him and tell me everything. Even if you think it isn't important. I need to know."

She nodded her head and then frowned, "And I'm not asleep. This isn't a dream?"

"No, you're very awake. In fact why don't you go make yourself a cup of coffee without the whiskey this time? I need you as alert as you can be."

"Yes, okay, um, do you drink coffee?" she asked turning back to look at me.

"No, thank you. I'm fine," I assured her and she hurried into the kitchen to fix her cup. I stood up and walked over to the mantle and picked up one of the many pictures of Pagan lined up on it. She was smiling brightly at the camera with her arms slung over the shoulders of Wyatt and Miranda. I rubbed the pad of my thumb over her sweet smile then put the picture back in its place.

"I just thought of something. Miranda's mother said Leif was in the car with her and he's missing too."

Without turning around to face her I replied, "Yes, I imagine so. Considering Leif is the son of Ghede."

Her loud gasp followed by the clatter of her cup hitting the tile floor reminded me I was dealing with a human here. One that, unlike Pagan, hadn't been seeing souls all her life. I really needed to monitor what I said more carefully.

Pagan

When I'd allowed myself to dwell on Ghede never once did I imagine what I was seeing at the head of the twenty-foot long table. Leaning back with a sinister grin on his face was a tall figure in a black top hat, a pair of dark sunglasses and two cigarettes hanging from his mouth. From what I could tell he was wearing a tuxedo with tails. Both of his feet were propped up on the table as he reclined in the enormous   carved marble and satin chair that reminded me more of a throne in a princess movie. Except, like most of the other items in the room, it was black.

Leif had placed us directly to the right of him and he was smiling proudly like he'd brought his prized possession to impress his father.

A scantily dressed woman placed a large silver cup in front of me and I was a little concerned her boobs were going to pop out in my face. I was terrified to drink or eat anything a bunch of voodoo spirits dined on but I also wanted to see Wyatt. So I forced myself to pick up the cup and lift it to my lips. The stench burned my nose and I quickly set it back down. There was no way I was drinking that.

Loud cackling laughter startled me and I jerked my attention from the offensive drink to see Ghede slap the table with one hand and laugh amazingly loudly without once dropping a cigarette from his mouth.

"She amuses me son," he bellowed and the rest of the attendees at the table joined in on his laughter.

Leif's hand reached for mine under the table in an attempt to squeeze it and I jerked it away quickly. I didn't want him to touch me.

"You don like de rum do ya gurl," Ghede stated for the rest of the table to hear.

Rum. So that was what it was. No, I didn't like the rum.

"No," I replied, unable to hold his piercing stare even with those dark glasses of his on. You could still feel it.

"Ah, we might need to fix dat."

Highly unlikely.

"Could she just have some soda, father?" Leif asked and for once I was thankful for his presence. My mouth was incredibly dry.

"Yes get de gurl some soda," he ordered one of the women standing back around the table waiting to do his bidding.

"Thank you," I managed to choke out. *Wyatt,* I reminded myself. I was doing this for Wyatt.

"Ah and she's got de manners. You chose good son. I lak dis one."

Leif beamed beside me and I felt the urge to gag.

"Dis one," Ghede announced loudly to the rest of the table, "she fell in love wit Dankmar. Das right," he enjoyed the surprised responses that came from the others. I peered down the table for the first time since sitting down and had to force myself not to openly gape at them. At least my dress didn't stand out. Every female at the table was dressed in a similarly ancient style of dress. However, their chests were much bigger so they really did have cleavage up to their nose. I sucked in a quick breath when I watched one of the men pull the front of a lady's dress until her entire breast bounced free. Swinging my eyes off them I studied the other side of the table. Men were all dressed in tuxedos and several even wore black masks. The hairstyles on the women were alarmingly high. Curls stacked up at least a foot with sparkling jewels, feathers, and other items stuck into the mix. They all drank liberally and laughed even shrilly. A loud squeal brought my eyes back to the other side of the table and I watched as the man who'd pulled the woman's top down now had her butt up on the edge of the table and was shoving her dress up, which was a feat all its own with all the fabric, and she was spreading her legs wide and squealing delightedly. When the man went to unbutton his bottoms I closed my eyes and snapped my head back around to look toward the wall behind Leif's head. Dear God, they were about to ... to *do it* at the table. What had I agreed to?

"Father please, Pagan isn't used to this sort of behavior. For tonight can you stop them?" Leif asked from beside me and I wanted to bury my face in his shoulder and start humming a song to drawn out the loud grunts coming from the man only a few feet down from me.

"Whut? De sex is part of de fun. You won me to go wit out de sex? Whut is a party wit out de enjoyment of de flesh, hmmm. Non dat is de answer."

The woman began to moan loudly and call out words I'd never heard before. Leif's arm came around my shoulder and I used his side and his arm as muffles for my ears while my eyes remained tightly shut.

"I'm sorry, Pagan," he whispered into my hair.

If he was really sorry he wouldn't have bribed me to come to this place. It wasn't a meal it was a ... a... freaking orgy. More moans had joined in and I cringed in horror as women called out vulgar suggestions and men screamed nasty descriptions. This was nothing like I'd imagined.

"Father please, may we be excused?" Leif asked.

"Hmph, I guess. I don want to stop my party. You take de gurl and I'll send de food to you."

Relieved, I jumped up being careful not to glance back down the table and let Leif lead me out of the room and back into the safety of the large hallway.

"Ohmygod," I whispered horrified. My mind would forever be traumatized.

"I'm sorry. I'd hoped since you were there father would contain that but--"

"But he's a sick pervert," I finished for him.

Leif started to open his mouth, but I cut him off.

"Don't. I don't care about what I'm supposed and not supposed to say about him here. That was the most revolting experience of my life. And you just let me walk right into it. No preparation or warning."

"Because if I'd told you that was a possibility you wouldn't have gone and Father would have punished you."

"And that wasn't punishment?"

"No, he finds that entertaining. He's the voodoo spirit over many things. Eroticism is one of them."

"Ugh, oh, ugh," I shook my head and started walking back toward the room that I'd been in earlier.

"Don't you want to see the library?" Leif asked.

I thought about what I'd just seen and the idea that the library probably contained ninety percent porn was a major turnoff for me. "No, I'd prefer to go bleach my eyeballs and ears," I snapped back at him.

"What about Wyatt?"

He'd used the power card. I stopped and glared back at him. I hated he had something to hold over my head. "If you were really sorry about tonight you'd send him to me."

Lief nodded, "Done. And I'll bring you food too. Normal food and a soda."

I didn't argue because I was sure once my stomach settled down from the disgusting scene I'd witnessed I would be hungry. It had been awhile since I'd eaten.

"You need to take the next right then it's the third door on the right," Leif instructed. I was good with directions so I hadn't needed his reminder but I nodded nonetheless and picked up my pace. I was now terrified of what I might witness in these hallways.

The door was a dark purple with a large black skull carved out of marble mounted in the center of it. I hadn't paid attention to that when we'd exited it earlier. I twisted the large heavy knob and stepped inside.

It was sad that this was comforting to me. Earlier I'd hated it. Now, after that horrid experience I decided I needed to get very well acquainted with this room because I wasn't leaving it again.

Glancing down at my dress I wanted it off. It reminded me of the other women and I felt dirty wearing it. However, I didn't see my other clothes anywhere and I wasn't about to get naked.

CHAPTER TWENTY- ONE

The door creaked open behind me and I turned expecting to see Leif with food but instead it was Wyatt. He closed the door behind him and a sad smile touched his lips. He was more solid than souls were supposed to be.

"Hey Pagan."

I stared at him as it registered that he'd just spoken to me in my head.

"Wyatt, I'm so sorry," I replied stepping closer to him.

"This isn't your fault Pagan. I didn't understand any of it at first but Leif has visited me several times and he's explained everything."

"No, it is my fault. If I'd just gone with him when he told me about my soul you'd have lived. But I didn't know. If I'd known they'd take someone else in my place I would have never stayed."

"You thought Death would fix it in time," he replied.

"Yes, I did. I guess you know about Dank now."

Wyatt nodded then reached out a hand and although I wasn't sure if mine would go through it or if he was a solid as he seemed I reached out to take his. The cold hard hand under mine surprised me.

"You aren't like other souls. They can't talk and they aren't solid."

"I believe it's because of where we are. Here Ghede makes things the way he wants them to be. I believe he... uh," Wyatt stopped talking and looked away. He almost seemed embarrassed and slowly tonight's dinner came back to me and I realized what he was trying to say.

"He uses souls as his entertainment?" I asked

Wyatt peered back at me and nodded. My stomach felt sick again. Had Ghede used Wyatt that way? I was going to throw up.

"No Pagan, he hasn't forced me to do any of ... that stuff. I've just seen it. I believe my age keeps me safe from it, I'm not sure."

I leaned against the side of the bed and sagged in relief.

"He intends to keep you here you know."

I lifted my eyes back to Wyatt's and nodded. "I know. I just wish there was a way I could get you out of here. It isn't fair that you have to remain here now that I agreed to come. He has me. I won't leave."

"How is Miranda?" Wyatt asked and the pain in his eyes sliced through me.

I remembered her sitting on her bed with his notes encircling her and the teddy bear he'd given her in her lap. I couldn't tell him how much she grieved his death. It would be too much.

"She's okay. She misses you something fierce but each day she gets better," I assured him.

His face fell, *"That was before. When she had you. Now she's lost us both."*

The unsaid words hanging in the air between us were thick and painful.

"She's stronger than you think," I assured him but the memory of her drunken body staggering out of the graveyard said another thing entirely.

"I hope so."

I could tell from his tone he didn't agree. He was right of course. Miranda was like a fragile flower. One that needed tending and special care. Wyatt had always understood that and gone out of his way to give her exactly what she needed. I'd loved him for that.

"He's coming," Wyatt said, staring at the closed door.

"Can you stay?" I asked, not ready to see him go.

"No. But I'll come back again."

"Stay. I'll ask him to let you."

Wyatt shook his head, *"I don't want to Pagan. I don't want to be near him."*

I understood. Leif had taken everything from Wyatt. His future. His eternity.

"Bye Pagan."

"Bye."

Leif opened the door and Wyatt walked past him without a word.

Frowning, Leif closed the door and walked over to the table beside the bed and set down a silver tray filled with recognizable items such as cheese and crackers, strawberries, dinner rolls, pulled pork and chocolate chip cookies.

"He isn't fond of me," Leif murmured as he handed me a large round porcelain plate.

"No,he isn't. But then who can blame him? You took away his eternity. He is now stuck here, forever." The anger lacing in my words caused him to flinch.

"I didn't take his soul Pagan, my father did. I had no idea he was going to. Ghede answers to no one within our realm. He makes decisions that please him and he overindulges in anything pleasurable and corrupts enjoyable pursuits, making things that should be good and satisfying into depraved behaviors. Nothing I can say will stop him. I was a child when he asked me to choose a soul. I had no idea what the implications were. I chose you. I didn't know then what that meant. You can hate me but try to understand I am not my father."

He may not be his father but he didn't have the courage to stand up to his father. He was weak but hadn't I always known that? Even back when I thought he was a human Leif had been weak. He never really accepted the weight of his actions. He always made you feel as if his apology were something precious and special that you would be stupid not to accept. The charisma he'd carried had won him many advances. Who was he exactly? If his father was Ghede then who was Leif?

"Who is your mother?"

Leif paused from fixing his plate. The strawberry in his fingers plopped onto his plate then he sighed wearily before raising his eyes to peer through his long blond eyelashes at me. "My mother is Erzulie, she is the reason my skin is pale and my hair is blond. She's the Voodoo Goddess of many things. Love being one... vengeance being another. She takes many lovers and enjoys the same things my father does. I see her on occasion but for the most part I live with my father. She has never had any desire for a child but then I'm not her only one. She has several, many of whom walk the earth. She is not above taking human men to her um... bed."

His mother was a deranged voodoo sex goddess. Great.

I stuffed some pulled pork into a dinner roll and chewed while I let this information sink in. I'd never really questioned his skin color until tonight. When I'd seen that his father was dark brown in coloring it had surprised me. But then I was a little shocked by the wild orgy going on and that kind of took precedence. After taking a long swig of the canned coke Leif had brought me I studied him a moment.

"You don't talk like your father either. He has a bit of a cajun accent."

Leif shrugged, "I've spent the majority of my life following you. I adopted your accent so I would fit in with your life. I didn't want to appear to you as an outsider."

"So all those dreams I've had are real? Those things really happened. Are there more memories I've forgotten?"

Leif stared intently at the food on his plate. Then managed a small shrug, "Maybe a few more."

He was lying. He couldn't even look at me. "A few more? That's all?"

Setting his plate on the table Leif stood up and began to pace at the end of the bed. I watched as I ate the cheese and crackers on my plate. I had a feeling I wasn't going to like this answer and I decided I'd better eat now before I lost my appetite again.

"I've been with you many times in your life. When you were lonely or sad, I was there. When you were in danger, I was there. It was what I did. Father said you were mine and I should protect you. So I did. I'm sorry that you don't remember. It wasn't something I did on purpose. It's just that I am soulless and your soul can't remember me for long when I'm not near you."

"Why did you want me to remember those times? The ones you'd picked out for me to dream about?"

Leif stopped pacing and placed his hands on the railing at the foot of the bed. His eyes bore into me. "Because those were the times I fell a little more in love with you."

No. Nonononono. I did not want him to love me. I wanted him to let me go. "You don't love me, Lief. If you loved me you'd never have been able to hold me against my will."

Leif growled in frustration and threw his hands up, "I've told you I can't control my father. He saved your life. He owns you Pagan."

"No one owns me."

Leif shook his head, "I don't want to argue with you. Not tonight. Let's just eat. Okay?" he walked back around and picked up his plate.

I finished eating my food until my stomach was finally satisfied and then drank every last drop of my coke. I wasn't sure how long it would be before I got a chance to eat again. Because there was no possible way I'd go back to that dining room. They could starve me for all I cared.

"Are you full?" Leif asked standing up and stacking our plates on the tray.

"Yes," that was the only reply he was going to get from me.

He turned to leave then stopped. His shoulders heaved with a heavy sigh and he looked back at me.

"What can I do to prove to you that I do love you? Anything except letting you go; because I can't. I'll do whatever else you ask of me. I want you to accept this. Us. Just tell me."

I stared back at him and I knew what I could do to make my eternity more bearable. "Release Wyatt to a transporter. Don't keep him here."

"If I can convince my father to release Wyatt to a transporter then you will believe I love you and you'll let this work between us?"

I felt the lump rise up in my throat at the promise I was about to make. I'd be throwing away the small hope that Dank could save me from this. But Wyatt's soul was at stake because of me. "Yes, if you hand Wyatt's soul over to a transporter and I get to see this happen. Once I know it has happened and that his soul is where it belongs then I will stay with you. I'll do whatever I can to make you happy. To make... us... happy."

Leif's face broke into a grin for the first time all night, "You have a deal. Get some rest Pagan. Tomorrow is a new day and I can't wait to start eternity with you."

I couldn't agree with him. I'd just shattered my own heart.

Dank

Standing in the crumbling school building left devastated by the tornado that had just taken out an entire town I couldn't focus on my purpose. I needed to be searching for the entrance to Vilokan. But souls had to be taken. I stalked through the grief stricken building pulling souls from the bodies of children and teachers. Several transporters followed in my wake. Each time I'd pass a child whose soul wasn't in need of release I was thankful. One more life that had been saved from this tragedy.

I continued on to each building and house no longer counting the souls as I took them. It only took moments and I was then walking across the muddy roads of Nicaragua taking souls from sick women and children who never stood a chance. Cardboard houses and dirt floors littered the land. No clean drinking water for miles. So much poverty here while other places had such an abundance.

Different countries, continents, causes all flashed before me as I snatched souls from bodies. Death happened often. It was a dark void I'd once walked with no joy. Then Pagan had entered my world and she'd made everything right. She'd made the emptiness leave and given me a reason to exist. Now, she was gone. I'd let her down. I'd lost her and I was on the brink of storming the streets of New Orleans and ripping it wide open until I found the portal I was looking for.

"Dankmar," Gee's voice called out to me and I spun around from my task and glared at her.

"What?" I snarled angrily. Seeing her only made me remember Pagan. My Pagan.

"Ghede is releasing Wyatt's soul to a transporter. The Creator has summoned me. He said to alert you and you could choose to do with that information what you liked."

"Where? When?" I asked as hope soared through my chest.

"Tonight. He wants it done as soon as possible."

Why? What was his game? "Where?" I demanded.

"Bourbon Street."

So the portal was on Bourbon Street.

"I need all transporters to go with us. You rally them. I'll handle the rest."

Gee ran to keep up with me as I stalked down the street toward the Catholic church where a priest had just ended his life. I'd deal with that soul then I'd call in the troops.

"Why? What're you gonna do?"

"I'm going to bust Hell wide open. That's what I'm going to do."

"You mean Vilokan?"

"Same thing."

CHAPTER TWENTY- TWO

Pagan

I was tired of this room. Even though the nurses were all really nice, I missed my bedroom. I loved my pink fluffy cover and my Bratz dolls. I'd asked mommy if we could go get them but she said it was too far away. She didn't want to leave me that long and I didn't want her to be gone long either. Now, that Grandma had gone back home to see her doctor it was just mommy and me. She'd gone to get some coffee and something hot to eat she'd said. I knew she didn't sleep very good in the chair beside me that turned into a bed. But I was glad she stayed. At night I would get scared. The room was so dark and then sometimes my door would open and no one would be there. Mommy said ghosts weren't real but I wasn't so sure.

I missed Grandma already. She read me a story every morning. I wanted to ask mommy to read me a story today but her eyes had looked so sleepy. I reached under my pillow and pulled out the pretty heart shaped pin Grandma had left me. I always loved it when she wore it on her fancy shirts. She said my grandfather had given it to her on their wedding day. He'd told her that now she had his heart. That was a silly thing to say but it sounded kind of sweet. I had it now because I had Grandma's heart. I could always remember she loved me.

The door opened and in stepped a guy I didn't know. He wasn't wearing white or blue so he wasn't a doctor or a nurse. His dark hair was kind of long in front and it curled a little on the end. Really blue eyes studied me and I stared right back. He had long eyelashes like a girl but he was wearing a black leather jacket and scruffy jeans and a pair of black boots so he wasn't very girly. Was he somebody's older brother and he'd got lost?

"Hello Pagan," he said in a warm deep voice that made me feel at ease.

"Hey. How do you know my name?"

He kind of laughed a little. "Because I'm here to talk to you about something."

"I'm not supposed to talk to strangers," I replied shaking my head and pointing my finger toward the door. Mommy would have a fit when she got back and found him in here.

"That's correct but I'm not exactly a stranger. You'll be seeing me again soon. I'm here to explain something to you and I need you to listen to me, okay?"

I nodded

"Your body is sick. The doctors aren't going to be able to make it better. But your body is just a shell. You are a soul. When this body gets too sick the soul will need to leave it and that's where I come in. I'll be here to take you out of this sick body and then I'll give you to a beautiful young girl who will remind you of a fairy princess. She'll take you to a place where you'll be given a new body."

"But how will my mommy know me if I'm in a different body? She just knows this body."

"That's true. You see, the life you have now will die. Do you remember when your grandfather died?"

I nodded

"Well, his soul left that body and he was sent up and given a new body. A new life. Your next life your soul will be near your mommy's soul and the souls of all the people you love. Souls are attached in each lifetime. You won't remember this life but your soul will remember the souls it loves."

So I wasn't going to have to go sit and wait on Mommy up in Heaven? I was going to get to come back and see her again?

"Okay."

The guy seemed happy with my reply. "Good girl. Now, the next time you see me you'll know it's time. You come with me. Don't try to stay with your body because you want to get another life, okay?"

I didn't understand really but I nodded. Then I remembered my grandma's pretty heart. I squeezed it tightly and asked, "Can you take this and give it to me after my soul leaves my body? I want to keep it."

The guy frowned and reached for the pink heart in my outstretched hand.

"I guess I could do that," he replied.

I watched as he slipped it into his jeans.

The door opened and in walked my mommy, "Hey sweetheart, I brought you some of that orange juice you like so much," she said in her happy voice. I

*glanced up at the guy and he put his finger over his
lips and shook his head and then he was gone.*

"What is this?" I asked holding up the strange silk gown I'd found on my bed when I'd woken up.

Leif sat down a tray filled with donuts, berries, cream, bagels, cream cheese, and bacon before answering me. "It's the ceremonial gown you'll wear tonight."

"Um no, I want my jeans."

Leif clenched his jaw and stood up straighter. "No, Pagan you will wear what I tell you to wear. I'm tired of you being so difficult. You agreed that if I made arrangements for Wyatt's soul to be handed over to a transporter you'd do everything you could to make this work."

Well, crap. "I didn't realize you would be picking out my wardrobe from now on is all," I grumbled and dropped the black gown back to the bed and reached for a cream filled donut.

"I know, and normally I won't be, but there are certain times you must wear certain things. This is one of those times. You'll be with me as my princess standing with Ghede."

"But it looks like a nightgown," I argued.

"It will look lovely on you," Leif replied.

I glanced back at the piece of offensive silk. Did everything Ghede have his hand in have to be so *sexual*?

242

"It will cover you properly. I promise. But you must get comfortable with your flesh. Here it is worshipped and appreciated. There are few who cover it up. The only coverings on the flesh are meant to enhance the attractiveness, not hide it."

I wanted my jeans. Now. Just hearing him talk about my flesh made my *flesh* crawl. If he expected me to flash my body for his perverted father he was crazy. I'd agreed to make this work not become a call girl.

"It all just takes some getting used to."

"When will we be giving Wyatt's soul to a transporter?" I really wanted a change of subject.

"This evening."

Good. I had hoped it would be today. Picking up the silver goblet I paused and lifted it toward Leif, "What's in this?"

"Grape juice. It's fresh and like nothing you've ever tasted," Leif replied with an amused grin.

Since I was here for eternity I had to start trusting him. I put the cup to my lips and took a tentative sip. The sweet juice hit my tongue and I quickly drank more. He was right. It was like nothing I'd ever put in my mouth. The rich taste awakened my taste buds and I felt a little lightheaded. Warning bells went off in my head and I quickly set the drink down and reached for the bowl of berries.

"It was a sugar rush, Pagan. Nothing more," Leif said as he reached for his cup.

I wasn't so sure about that but then I was also paranoid. With good cause.

"Would you like a visit from Wyatt before he leaves?"

"Yes, please." I'd managed to sound polite that time.

It obviously pleased Leif because he smiled a little too brightly.

I finished with my breakfast and hoped Leif would take that as a hint to leave. He'd knocked and woken me up asking if I wanted breakfast then given me barely enough time to pull on the robe he'd supplied last night with my pajamas. Which were flannel, thank God.

I'd had a dream last night of a memory that absolutely nothing to do with Leif. He hadn't been in my head. I'd dreamed of the day Dank had come to my hospital room and I'd given him my brooch. Tears burned my eyes as I thought about the brooch that now lay beside my bed at home. It was the one thing I wished I'd been able to bring with me.

"I'll take this tray away and come back for you soon. Maybe we can finally take that tour," Leif said in a jovial tone. He had so much to be happy about. He'd won.

"Could you send Wyatt to see me?" That was all I really cared about.

Leif nodded, "Of course."

He closed the door behind him and I stared at it hating the sight of it and wondering if this was ever going to get better.

CHAPTER TWENTY- THREE

"You convinced them to let me go," Wyatt's voice entered my head and I spun around to see him standing in my doorway.

"Yes, it's the least I can do."

"But what about you? What did you promise them to get them to agree to this?"

"Nothing I wouldn't have to do anyway. I'm stuck here Leif. I just promised I wouldn't be an eternal brat if they granted me this one wish."

Wyatt smiled, *"You do know how to be a brat."*

"Look who's talking 'Mr. No Girls Allowed.'"

Wyatt's grin grew, *"You aren't ever going to let that go are you?"*

"Nope and I have an eternity to simmer about it."

His amused grin faded. I hadn't meant to remind us both what I was in store for.

"I wish I could take you with me," his voice had dropped to a whisper.

"Me too. But this is it. It's my fate. It isn't yours and I'm so thankful you're being set free."

"Do you think Death... er, Dank will come?"

I doubted Ghede would let him get close to me if he did. Besides what good would it do? I couldn't allow Death to take me. Ghede would take the life of someone else I loved and we'd be back in this same predicament.

"Doesn't matter if he does. I must pay this restitution."

Wyatt shook his head in frustration. *"This is so wrong."*

I couldn't agree more but I was going to come to terms with it. I forced a smile.   "Would you do something for me?"

"Of course," he quickly replied.

"Would you tell Dank that I will always love him? That I'm sorry that I can't leave here. I'm protecting those I love. But I will think of him every day and I will hum his song to myself every night as I go to sleep."

Wyatt nodded then smirked, *"That's kind of too mushy for my taste but yeah, I guess I can relay that."*

I rolled my eyes at him and he chuckled. It was almost as if we were sitting across from each other in the cafeteria again.

"He's returning and you know how I feel about him."

"I love you Wyatt. I'm going to miss you," I called out as he opened the door.

He stopped and looked back at me, *"I love you too Pagan. I'll miss you too. In every life."*

Sniffling, I managed to nod before he disappeared out the door.

Dank

"You know Dankmar, when you told me we were going to handle everything else I kind of thought maybe you were going to get backup. But a bunch of transporters and you aren't enough to shut down an entire voodoo posse."

I had a plan but for once Gee didn't need to know everything. She'd done what I asked of her and that was enough.

"I got this," I simply replied

"I'm hoping you know something I don't know because not only are we about to confront a bunch of voodoo spirits but we're also going to do it on their turf. Right here in their mecca. You ever heard the saying, 'home field advantage' well, this is the description."

"I got this Gee."

With a weary sigh she trudged on beside me with the hundreds of transporters in our wake. We kind of looked like the devil with heavenly host groupies but I didn't care. My plan was sound. This was going to work or I really would charge Vilokan and take down every spirit who stood in my way. They'd asked for my fury; well, now they had it.

Pagan

The door swung open after one swift knock, "It's time," Leif announced smiling brightly.

I really wanted to slap the smile off his face but instead I adjusted the black *nightgown* that I was being forced to wear and thanked my lucky stars it was long. "Let's do this," I replied and headed for the door. He offered his arm and I shook my head, "No, it's not over yet. You get Wyatt safely in a transporter's hands and out of this place, then I'll hold up my end of the deal.

Leif seemed to think about that a moment then nodded. At least he was reasonable.

"You lead the way," I said standing back once we were out in the hallway. I had no clue where we were going.

"You know that Dankmar will probably be here, Pagan."

Yes, I'd already prepared myself for that. The urge to run into his protective arms was going to be strong but I had to keep my head. Lives depended on me. Lives of those I loved.

"I figure he would be," I replied icily.

"You understand the implications if you go to him."

"Yes Leif, I know you'll kill off everyone I love and suck their souls down here to live in fornication for all eternity. Got it."

Leif stopped and turned back to look at me. "Pagan, this isn't about me. I've told you this is my father. It's how he operates. I can't control him. You have no idea how much cajoling I had to do in order for him to give Wyatt's soul back. And to be honest the only reason I think he agreed is because he sees

248

entertainment value in you refusing to go to Dankmar and that he will be the one controlling you."

I felt sick at my stomach. I really hated his father.

"Now please understand, no pain you have suffered is because I wanted it. I never wanted you to hurt. I always thought you'd want me. That your soul would want me. Hell when I get anywhere near you your eyes look like they've caught on fire. You're supposed to want me. But you don't. Instead you want him. And you can't have him, Pagan. It was never meant to be."

I opened my mouth to scream at him how unfair all of this was but quickly snapped it closed again. I needed to stop being angry with him. This was my life now. At some point I had to accept it. Today would be a good day.

"Okay."

Leif raised an eyebrow, "Okay?"

"You heard me, Leif. I said okay. Now let's go."

He looked a little taken aback but he nodded then continued to lead the way. We turned down one masked hall to another until two large doors up ahead were opened wide and I could see the familiar sight of Bourbon Street.

We walked by other inhabitants I recognized from dinner last night and I cringed as they smiled sadistically at me. I was stuck with these sickos.

"Stop it," Leif hissed as one of the men ogled my chest area.

He pulled me up against him and I went gladly.

"May, dat is sumtin to see is it not," Ghede called out as he walked into the large foyer. He was once again in a top hat, black sunglasses, and a tuxedo with tails.

"Don't make her uncomfortable, Father," Leif pleaded.

"Who me?" he asked in an amused voice. I watched as he lifted his hand and placed two cigarettes in his mouth and then turned his attention to the activities going on outside. I'd seen this once and I didn't want to watch again.

Wyatt walked into the room flanked on either side by practically naked women. Which wasn't surprising; I was beginning to think every female down here but me liked to wear as little as possible.

One of the women ran a long red fingernail down the middle of Wyatt's shirt and then continued on down over his zipper. He didn't flinch but I could see the tension in his face.

"Please make them stop," I whispered to Leif who followed my gaze.

He shook his head and leaned down to me, "If I make a scene Father will then make it much worse. If you don't want to see one of those two mount Wyatt right here then don't say a word. Wyatt knows this. That's why he's so still."

Swallowing the bile in my throat burned and I had to turn my eyes away from them and pray the transporter wasn't late.

The streets outside suddenly became vacant and quiet.

"Ah, Death draws near. The fallen have run to hide," Ghede drawled and pulled the two cigarettes from his mouth to exhale small rings of smoke before placing them right back in.

"What does he mean?," I asked Leif

"Dank is close. The souls of the people in the streets felt him and ran. Unlike you most humans don't cling to Death when he's in his true form. Sure, they like the singer Dank Walker but when he's truly in Death's form they hide."

I watched as the dark streets grew brighter. Whispers and giggles behind me had me wanting to run out in the road away from all this but Wyatt stirred to my left and I remembered why I was doing this. He gave me a sad smile and then Ghede beckoned him forward.

Dank, along with more transporters than I'd ever seen, filled the street in front of the doors. Gee was directly beside him. Her fierce expression scanned the crowd inside and immediately found me. I shook my head at her letting her know I couldn't come to them. If they'd brought all these transporters to take me then they were out of luck because I wasn't going. I couldn't.

"Well, well, well, Dankmar and pals. To wat do we owe dis honor?" Ghede asked in a loud amused voice.

"You know why I'm here, Ghede," Dank replied, locking his expression on me. The hard cold determination in his eyes transformed to fury as his gaze took in my dress.

"Tsk tsk tsk, I don know whut you mean. You said to let her choose," Ghede announced brightly waving his hand in my direction. "She did."

Gee took a step toward me and Dank's arm shot out and held her back. He understood. She didn't but he did.

"No. You forced her choice. That wasn't part of the deal," Dank replied. The venom in his voice caused me to shiver. I'd never heard him sound quite so sinister.

"Here's the soul you came for," Ghede pushed Wyatt toward Dank and Wyatt gladly went. A transporter stepped forward and instantly she and Wyatt's soul were gone.

"Now is dat all you want or would you lak to axe her yourself?" Ghede turned and beckoned me forward, "Come here Pagan," he coaxed.

Lief squeezed my arm and pushed me gently toward his father. I tried to remind myself that if I acted in any way like I was scared Dank would take me and be done with it. Then I'd lose someone else. I had to remain calm.

"Axe her Dankmar," Ghede goaded pushing me in front of him.

Dank's eyes bore into mine. He was trying to tell me something but I wasn't sure what. Instead, I closed my eyes tightly and fought for strength then opened them and stared straight at him. "I want--"

"I didn't ask you anything just yet Pagan. Hold onto that thought just a moment more," he cut me off. His hard glare drilled into Ghede who stood behind me.

"You've messed with the wrong guy this time Ghede. You like your entertainment but I was never one to entertain."

Transporters began to shift off to the sides covering the streets as massive men with actual swords hanging from their waists filled the street behind and beside Dank. Gasps and screeches and other horrified sounds came from behind me but I stood in amazement as the army around Dank grew.

"You brought de warriors for a gurl?" Ghede's voice sounded incredulous.

"Yes," was Dank's only reply. He took a step forward and held out his hand to me. I wanted to grab it and run to him but I shook my head as tears filling my eyes. "I can't," I choked.

"Trust me," he replied. I'd heard those exact same words from Leif so many times over the past few weeks but nothing he'd done had been trustworthy. Dank was different. He was Death. He knew the reasons why I was scared to leave. But his "trust me" was enough. I stepped forward and placed my hand in his. He pulled me up against his side.

"Bad choice leetle gurl," Ghede hissed from the other side of the door.

"No, Ghede. You're the only one who made the bad choice. You don't take what's mine."

Dank bent his head and kissed my temple. "I love you and I got this. No one else will die. Trust me. Now I want you to go with Gee and stand back out of the way," he whispered in my ear.

I nodded but quickly threw my arms around his neck and squeezed him tightly before Gee's hand wrapped around my arm.

"Come on you. There will be plenty of time for that later," Gee said tugging on me to come with her. I let go of Dank and hurried to keep up with her before she pulled my arm out of its socket.

"You took a soul that was too young to defend itself. A soul that belonged to the Creator. You changed fate and then decided to play with a world that is not yours. You stepped out of your realm and took another soul not under your rule. Now I give you a choice Ghede. We close this portal today as well as the ones found in Africa and Haiti where the warriors are now standing guard and we seal them for all eternity. Voodoo power will end right here. Right now. You crossed a line." Dank's loud commanding voice boomed over the streets. Even though I was over to the side further away from the opening and where Dank stood I had a clear view of the inside of Vilokan. Ghede's amused smirk was gone.

"Or you let Pagan's soul go. Free of any restitution. You stay clear of her and her family for all eternity and remain as you are. But I warn you if I see your son, you or any of your spirits again remotely close to Pagan I will end this religion. There will be no second chances. It's your choice."

Ghede turned and stared back at Leif whose gaze met mine. His father was letting him choose. I felt a small touch of sympathy for the boy who'd been in my life for so many years. I knew there were memories I'd never remember where Leif had come into my life when I needed someone. I was thankful for those times. If only he'd been the honest, pure, sweet guy that he'd seemed. But he was a product of evil. Nothing would ever change that. He was selfish and weak. He would never be enough for me. My heart could never love him. My soul could never want him.

Then he replied, "Let her go."

CHAPTER TWENTY- FOUR

Dank

The wispy pink fabric brushed against her legs as she made her way toward me. I enjoyed the view of her entrance rather than going to her. Strappy silver heels encased her small dainty feet. The hem of the dress brushed her skin right above her knees. The waistline was high and the chiffon was belted with a wide satin sash. Directly over her heart the familiar filigree heart twinkled as the lighting hit each small pink stone. There were no straps and the soft skin of her shoulders were visible as was her elegant neckline. Normally, I enjoyed her hair down but there was something to be said for having all that mass of brown silk piled up high on her head leaving her neck and shoulders bare.

When she was only steps away I moved toward her and held out my hand. She slipped her hand into mine and the connection of our palms sent warmth flooding through me. The light charcoal that outlined her eyes caused the green to stand out more. I was taken away by the depth of her beauty as she gazed up at me. After taking in every perfect part of her appearance as she entered the room it would almost seem impossible for her soul to exceed her outward beauty. But as I soaked in the beautiful soul I saw so clearly through the window of her eyes I knew it did.

"Dank, we got to get on stage bro. If she's here then let's go," Loose, my drummer, interrupted me. Scowling, I swung my gaze around to meet his. The long blond dread locks the girls were so crazy about were pulled back in a ponytail tonight. I was tempted to reach over and jerk one out of his head.

Pagan had just arrived. Her mother had dropped her off for me. She'd been spending extra time with Miranda and her mother since her return. Both seemed to need reassurance that she was in fact alive. When she'd "washed up" on the shore a few miles away after her accident her memory had been temporarily gone. Well, that was our story. Leif was believed to have drowned. Although the memory of him would fade away soon enough. Many people were already forgetting him.

"I'm just saying it's time," Loose whined.

Pagan giggled beside me, "It's okay. Go on and rock the house."

I slipped my hand through hers and pulled her with me,"Not without you up there so I can see you." This was her prom too but I didn't like the idea of other guys dancing with my girl. She looked entirely too gorgeous tonight.

"No complaints from me," she chirped and followed me backstage.

We stopped to the left of the stage and I kissed her softly on the lips. I'd only meant to drop a quick peck but her arms wrapped around my neck and she nibbled against my bottom lip and I decided the crowd could wait.

Pulling her against me I enjoyed the sweet taste that was only Pagan. Her soft lips molded under mine and I fought to stay focused waiting on the moment her soul would release. A soft moan escaped her throat and my blood began to heat under each small lick and teasing touch from her tongue. Concentrating was becoming more difficult.

Pressing her soft chest against mine caused a shiver to run through me and a low growl began in my chest. Why wasn't her soul releasing yet? I couldn't keep this up or I'd completely lose all train of thought. Warm fingers grazed my abs as she worked a hand underneath my shirt.

Panting, I pulled back and stared down at her heavy eyelids and swollen lips. "Your soul, it isn't releasing," I managed to croak out.

Sliding her hand up higher on my chest she grinned wickedly up at me, "I noticed that too. Why did you stop?"

Had Leif's claim on her soul been affected it? Shaking my head I decided at the moment I didn't care. I wasn't going to turn down this unexpected gift. I reached down and picked her up then began taking long strides toward the back room where we'd left all the storage containers for our equipment.

"What are you doing?"

"I'm going to enjoy a long overdue make-out session with my girl. That's what I'm doing," I explained, stepping into the room and closing the door behind me with one shove of my foot.

"Oh," she gasped before I pressed her up against the wall, wrapping her legs around my waist and feasting on her mouth for the first time ever with nothing crowding my thoughts but how incredibly lucky I was.

Pagan

Dank's band sung four of their more popular songs and the Breeze High School graduating class of 2012 was loving every minute of it. We only had two more months until we walked across that stage and received our diplomas.

"Hey gorgeous, you're all kinds of distracting," Dank drawled in the dark smooth voice I loved so much. Loose was telling the crowd they'd be back after a ten minute break. I wrapped my arms around his waist and rested my head on his chest.

"You guys sounded awesome out there," I told him then tilted my head back to stare at his ridiculously perfect face.

"Les is a little off tonight but I think it's all the girls screaming out our names and the fact they're so close. Normally there is more distance between us and them and seeing who the screams belong to is hard if not impossible."

"Hmmm, so you're telling me Les is checking out the chicks?"

Dank chuckled, "That is one way to put it."

"I could probably make a few introductions for him if he is really interested"

Dank shook his head, "No, please don't. I want to keep these guys in a small section of my life. Not around me all the time. The last thing I need is for one of them to start dating a girl in Breeze."

I liked that this part of his life was off to the side in its own little box section. I already shared him with... the dead. I didn't want to share him with anyone else.

"You want to dance... or maybe go back to that storage room again?" he asked reaching behind his back to take both my hands in his.

"Yes to the dancing and yes to the storage room. In that order please," I replied feeling my skin heat up at the memory of having Dank's hands on me again.

We didn't walk down to the crowded dance floor. Dank pulled me up against him and began to sing in my ear as he twirled me around in our own little private spot, tucked away backstage. This was by far the best prom any girl had ever gone to.

*   *   *

"Haven't we been to every store in this mall already?" I moaned as my feet began to rebel.

Miranda glanced back at me and frowned, "We need the perfect dress and shoes to wear under our graduation gowns. We have to take them off and head to the party my dad is hosting for us directly after the ceremony. I'd think with your hot rocker boyfriend singing up on stage and all the girls fawning over him you'd want to make sure you looked hot."

Dank had not only had Cold Soul sing at our Prom he was now agreeing to bring them to our graduation party. Of course I was more than positive Miranda's father was paying them well. Dank had to pay the boys something. It was how they supported themselves.

I sank down on the nearest bench and took a big whiff of the cream cheese pretzels in the bakery directly across from me. It was the most heavenly smell on the face of the earth. Or at least right at this moment.

"Okay, if you go get me one of those yummy pretzels with the sweet cream cheese filling I'll continue to torture my feet in the search for perfection."

Miranda rolled her eyes, "Fine. But you have to share. They smell incredible and I don't need to eat a whole one by myself. Last thing I need is a belly while trying on dresses."

Miranda had never even come close to having a belly. It was my turn to roll my eyes. The girl was a nut.

I shoved a ten dollar bill at her and leaned back in the seat, "Please just go buy one. Heck, buy two. I'll eat one and a half."

"No, you won't. Remember you have the hot sexy boyfriend you need to look incredible for. One and a half of those one thousand calorie pretzels is not a move in the right direction."

"It's mostly pretzel Miranda. Those are fat free," I reminded her.

She opened her mouth to argue then snapped it closed before spinning around and marching off to the bakery.

She was back to her old self. It had taken awhile but she was definitely back. Some days she wanted to talk about Wyatt. Other days she couldn't bear to bring up his name. I just felt her out and went with her mood. Watching her stand with her hip cocked to one side and her hand placed on it as she waited impatiently made me smile. Her spunk was back.

An attractive guy turned around and noticed her. He spoke to her and looked to be offering to let her go first. But she didn't budge and her posture remained stiff. The guy looked a little let down that she'd blown him off and turned back around.

She wasn't completely back to normal and maybe she never would be. The old Miranda would have flirted her way to the front of the line. This one could hardly stand the sight of the opposite sex.

"Is this seat taken?" a warm sexy drawl asked and I lifted my gaze and smiled up at Dank.

"Yes. I'm saving it for my smoking hot boyfriend," I replied teasingly.

Dank slid in beside me and put his arm around my shoulder. "Hmmm, well he should have got here sooner. You snooze, you lose."

Giggling, I snuggled up to his side. "Save me from Miranda. She's trying to kill me via shopping."

"Impossible. I happen to know Death has a thing for you and you can't be killed off that easily."

I pinched his washboard abs through his t-shirt. It felt so good to be close to him and not have to worry about anything but normal teenage stuff like a best friend who has got part of her groove back and is now wearing me out.

"You ever find out anything about Wyatt?" I asked quietly peering up at him.

He nodded, "Yeah. Um, let's just say his death was an abnormal... er unique event. So his return is just as unique."

"What?" I asked sitting up so I could read his facial expression better.

Dank reached over and tucked a strand of hair behind my ear. "Just wait. You'll understand soon enough."

"Ahem, excuse me lovebirds but this is a shopping emergency day and I have our fuel. Now Dank, you need to run along and go be all smoldering and sexy somewhere else. I need all Pagan's attention today," Miranda had taken on a slightly bossy tone.

Dank kissed my mouth softly then cupped my face and whispered, "I love you," in my ear before standing up and leaving me in a puddle of mush on the bench.

"See ya later Miranda. Don't wear her completely out," Dank teased as he turned to walk away. I glanced over at Miranda who was watching his butt in awe and I swung my shopping bag to slap her in the side.

"HEY," she shrieked as she stumbled sideways.

"Stop looking at my boyfriend's butt," I replied to her scowl. I realized that maybe it was just guys who showed interest in her that she was opposed to. Those like Dank she didn't view as a betrayal she still checked out.

Biting her lip, she tried to keep from smiling, "Sorry, it's really hard not to."

"Well, *try*."

"Spoilsport," she muttered and grabbed my arm to pull me up.

"Let's walk and eat. I want to go see if they have a see through strapless bra at Victoria's Secret."

Groaning, I let her pull me up and grabbed my half of the pretzel from her hand. At least I had a treat to get me through this.

Dank

I went to open Pagan's bedroom door when someone cleared their throat behind me. I hadn't been careful and had gotten a little too comfortable with sneaking into her room in the morning. I'd have to face the music for that mistake. Turning around I found Pagan's mom standing across the hall with her hands on her hips and her eyebrows raised. Her dark brown hair was a little mussed from sleep but she was already in her work clothes: sweat pants and a teeshirt. Complete with coffee stain.

"Good morning," I tried to sound as polite as possible. It wasn't like she could keep me from coming to Pagan's room whenever I wanted but I still didn't want to have her as an enemy.

"Good morning, Dank. To what do we owe this early visit?"

This time I cleared my throat, "I thought I'd wake Pagan up. Don't want her to miss breakfast." Okay, that sounded lame.

"Really? Well, just so we're clear, I realize my daughter's boyfriend is ... well... something that isn't exactly human. But I still expect you to follow my rules."

"Of course," I replied.

She stared at me a moment longer then started to walk down the stairs. I stood frozen not sure if she wanted me to actually leave.

Stopping and glancing back over her shoulder at me she smiled, "Come on. I'll feed you while you wait." She then continued down the stairs and I smiled to myself while I followed her. Who was I to disobey her mom?

Once we got in the kitchen her mother opened a cabinet and got down the pancake mix, a large bowl and a spoon. "Here read the directions and start mixing up my batter while I get the griddle hot," she directed as she shoved the items into my arms.

I hadn't planned on cooking breakfast with Pagan's mother but it was past time she and I talked.

Our last private conversation had been the night I'd confronted her about Pagan's soul.

"The key to getting pancakes just the way Pagan likes them is to use a lot of butter. Real butter. It makes the edges crisp." I filed that piece of information away to use on a later date.

"When she was little I'd make her pancakes into the shape of Mickey Mouse. Well, his head at least. She loved them. She'd make eyes and a nose and a mouth with fruit and then cover it all with syrup."

I remembered the green eyes too big for her face staring up at me from the hospital bed that day I'd gone to talk to her. She'd lost all her hair and her face was frail and thin but her mind had been sharp as a tack. After that day I'd always remembered her when I walked into the rooms of dying children to explain to them what was to come. Her face had always come to mind and I'd wondered what had happened with that soul. Even then she'd had a sort of hold on me.

Her mother took the bowl from my hands. Luckily I'd managed to stir the milk, eggs, and mix together properly. Her approving nod was oddly relieving.

"So Dank Walker, you ever going to tell me exactly what you are?"

I'd wondered if now that Pagan was home, safe and sound, free of voodoo spirits that wanted her soul, her mother would ever question me about my admission that I wasn't human.

Clearing my throat I leaned a hip against the counter and crossed my arms over my chest. I wasn't sure she really wanted the answer to this question.

"Well, that depends on if you really want me to tell you. It might be best if you just know that I will protect her for all eternity. She'll never have to fear *death*." I stopped on that last word and waited. Her mother had just poured some batter onto the sizzling griddle and she froze for a moment then slowly lowered the bowl and spoon to the counter. Her head turned as if in slow motion until her eyes were staring incredulously into mine.

"Are you saying... I mean you can't be... are you saying... no, no that can't be right," she shook her head and gave me one last small frown before turning her attention back to the pancake in front of her. She flipped it then placed it on a plate and handed it to me.

"First one is always the best. Why don't you get started... that is if you... do you eat?"

I didn't hide my amusement as I reached for the plate. "Yes, I eat. Eternity would be awfully boring without food."

CHAPTER TWENTY-FIVE

Pagan

My mother's laughter carried up the stairs as I peeled open my eyelids and stared at the alarm clock that hadn't gone off this morning. Probably because I hadn't set it but that was just details. A low voice carried up the stairs and my mother's high pitched voice began chatting away again. She wasn't on the phone. Someone was here.

Sitting straight up in bed I covered my mouth. Had my mom let Roger sleep over? She'd never in all my life had a boyfriend sleep over. Swinging my legs over the side of the bed I grabbed my short yellow bathrobe and hurried out the door to catch her red-handed. It wasn't that I cared really. It would just be fun to hold over her head.

Running down the steps taking two at a time I hit the bottom step and took off around the corner then came skidding to a halt. Seated at my kitchen table with a pile of pancakes and bacon filling the plate in front of him was Dank. His dark curls were perfectly messy and the pale blue shirt I'd convinced him to buy because it would make his eyes stand out even more hugged his well-defined chest. A touch of humor lit his eyes and his lips were in a sexy little smirk that was so incredibly kissable. Kissable was exactly what I was supposed to be enjoying this morning. Last I'd spoken with Dank he was going to wake me up with kisses.

I shifted my gaze to my mother who sat smiling as if she knew a secret with her hands both cupping what was probably her fourth cup of coffee today. She'd tucked her unstyled hair behind her ears and her glasses were perched on her nose like a school teacher.

"What are y'all doing?" I asked incredulously.

"We're eating breakfast and talking. Which you could be doing if you'd get up on time," my mother replied with a little tartness to her tone. It drove her nuts that I slept so late.

"These pancakes are really good, Pagan. I can't believe you don't get up early enough to enjoy these every morning," Dank piped in.

I glowered at him, "Is that so?"

He nodded as he stuck another forkful into his mouth. The traitor. He'd passed up coming in my room to wake me up for my mother's pancakes.

"I hope you enjoy your pancakes. I'm going to go get ready now since my alarm clock didn't wake me up on time. Must have been preoccupied with something else." I snapped and headed back up the stairs. My mother's smothered laughter told me that maybe my alarm clock had gotten derailed from his mission by the mothership.

"Stinking pancakes," I muttered and went to get a shower.

*   *   *

It felt like only yesterday I'd walked into this gym for the first time. Freshman orientation had been so exciting yet terrifying. Miranda and I had sat on the fourth row left side bleachers holding hands tightly as Principal Cagle welcomed us and read us our rights. Wyatt had sauntered in late and taken the spot beside me. We'd all been so young. I'd even met Jay that day. He was a sophomore and on the basketball team. He'd come up to us and introduced himself to Wyatt asking if he was planning on playing basketball. He'd seen Wyatt play in middle school. We'd won the state championship last year. Wyatt was just that good. Then Jay had asked if I was Wyatt's girlfriend and we'd all laughed as if that was the funniest thing we'd ever heard. Two weeks later Jay had asked me out on our first date.

Memories were thick as I gazed around at all my classmates. We all wore the same royal blue robes and we all wore the same expression. Relief, excitement, and just a touch of uncertainty. We'd walked into this building not knowing what groups we'd fit into, what teachers were the best, and what meals we should never eat in the cafeteria. Now we knew all those things and more.

On my last day in this gym, I was sitting between two of the most important people in my world once again. Miranda held my right hand and Dank held my left hand. Although, Miranda was squeezing my right hand so tightly I was afraid of damage from blood loss and Dank was more caressing my left hand with the pad of his thumb.

Even sitting between them I couldn't help but feel a little bereft. We were missing one important piece of the puzzle. Wyatt should have been here too. I knew Miranda was thinking the same thing. That was why I didn't mention the fact she was crushing the bones in my hand. I figured if my right hand would help her get through this then I'd gladly sacrifice it.

"You okay?" Dank whispered in my ear.

I nodded and laid my head over on his shoulder.

The guest speaker finished his speech followed by the Valedictorian, Krissy Lots. Once she finished we went one at a time as our names were called to receive our diplomas. Whistles and catcalls erupted all over as different students took the stage.

"Pagan Annabelle Moore"

I got a squeeze from both Miranda and Dank's hands as I went to the stage. Clapping followed by a whistle coming from Dank and a loud 'woot' coming from Miranda brought a smile to my face. As I took my diploma, I crossed the stage and another cheer from the back of the gym caught my attention. Glancing back I saw Jay leaning against the door clapping and smiling brightly. I wondered if he'd come back because he knew it would be difficult with Wyatt's absence. Smiling in his direction I made my way off the stage and over to my seat.

"You have a fan in the back," Dank said in a cold unamused tone when I sat back down.

"Oh no, it's just Jay. I didn't know he was going to be here today."

Dank's jaw tensed and he turned to glare in Jay's direction. Oh my, this wasn't good. Jealous Dank could be dangerous. I pulled on Dank's arm, "It's okay. Really. I think he probably came because of Wyatt's not being here. To, you know, show support. They were close."

Dank's eyes went from angry to slightly surprised as his gaze stayed directed over my shoulder. Curious, I turned my head and saw a tall guy with shaggy light brown hair that curled up around the bottom and an orange UT polo shirt standing beside Jay. They were talking and Jay was smiling at whatever the guy was saying. He must have brought one of his frat brothers. Then the guy turned to look our way and a strange peace came over me. It was an odd thing. Not something I'd ever felt with a stranger before. His gaze met mine and he smiled. Then he turned his attention to Miranda who wasn't even looking their way. He had an almost reverent expression on his face. I watched them a moment then turned back around in my seat.

"Pagan," Dank whispered beside me.

"Hmm," I replied leaning in so I could hear him better.

"Remember when I told you Wyatt's return would be unique?"

"Yes."

"Well, he's back."

Frowning I lifted my eyes to meet his, "Who's back?"

Dank's eyes shifted over my shoulder back to the door where the boys were standing and then back to me. "Wyatt. His soul is back."

EXISTENCE
TRILOGY

"Yet You Stay" by Dank Walker has been recorded and can be bought at iTunes.

Read excerpts retold in Dank's point of view from Existence exclusively at www.abbiglines.com

Keep up with all current contest, giveaways, and special Existence Trilogy releases (such as Predestined excerpts retold in Leif's point of view) at the Existence Trilogy Facebook page.

I've listed my upcoming releases in the last few pages of this book. Book #3 has a title and a release date. Be sure to check it out.

My official playlist for **Predestined**- these are the songs that inspired the story:

Novocaine for the Soul by Eels
Be My Angel by Mazzy Star
Fade Into You by Mazzy Star
Tear You Apart by She Wants Revenge
My Heart by Paramore
What It is to Burn by Finch
One Last Breath by Creed
Your Guardian Angel by Red Jumpsuit Apparatus
Savin' Me by Nickelback
Run by Leona Lewis
My Last Breath by Evanescence

Also by Abbi Glines

BECAUSE OF LOW

CHAPTER ONE

Marcus

Moving back home sucked. Everything about this town reminded me of why the hell I'd wanted to get away. I had a life in Tuscaloosa and I needed that life to escape. Here, I was Marcus Hardy. No matter where I went people knew me. They knew my family. And now... they were talking about my family. Which is why I had come home.

Leaving my sister and mother here alone to face this was impossible. The scandal hovering over our heads took away all my choices and my freedom. Right now, few people knew but it was only a matter of time. Soon the entire coastal town of Sea Breeze, Alabama would know what my dad was doing or should I say, who my dad was doing. King of the Mercedes car dealerships along the Gulf Coast had been a high enough title for some little gold digging whore only a few years older than me to jump in bed with my dear 'ol dad. The one time I'd seen the home wrecker working behind the desk right outside Dad's office I'd known something wasn't right. She was young and smoking hot and apparently money hungry.

Dad couldn't keep it in his pants and now my mom and sister would have to deal with the stigma it would cause. People would feel sorry for Mom. This was already devastating to her and she didn't even know yet that the other woman was barely a woman. My younger sister Amanda had caught them going at it one evening late when Mom had sent her over to the office to take Dad some dinner. She'd called me that night crying hysterically. I'd withdrawn from school, packed my things and headed home. There was no other option. My family needed me.

A knock on the door snapped me out of my internal tirade and I went to see what chick was here looking for Cage this time. God knew the guy had an endless line of females parading through his life. My new roommate was a player. A major player. He put my best friend, Preston, to shame. I twisted the knob and swung the door open without peeking through the hole.

The surprise was on me. I'd been prepared to tell whatever tall willowy large but obviously fake chested female dressed in almost nothing waiting outside the door that Cage was busy with another one very similar to her. Except a very natural almost curvy red head stood before me. Red rimmed eyes and a tear streaked face gazed up at me. There was no mascara lines running down her face. Her hair wasn't styled but pulled back in a pony tail. She wore jeans and what appeared to be an authentic Back in Black

AC/DC concert t-shirt. No belly button flashing a flat tanned stomach and her clothes weren't skin tight. Well maybe the jeans were a little snug but they hugged her hips nicely. My appreciation of her legs in the slim fit jeans stopped however when I noticed the small beat up suitcase clutched tightly in her hand.

"Is Cage here?" Her voice sounded broken and musical at the same time. I was having a hard time digesting that this girl was here for Cage. She wasn't anything like he veered toward. Nothing was enhanced. Everything from her thick dark copper hair to the Chuck Taylors on her feet screamed, "not Cage's type." And the fact she was carrying a suitcase, well that couldn't be good.

"Uh, um, no."

Her shoulders slumped and another sob escaped her mouth. One small dainty hand flew up in an attempt to mute the sound of her obvious distress. Her nails were even classy. Not too long with a smooth rounded tip and soft pink nail polish.

"I left my cell phone," she let out a sigh then continued, "at my sister's. I need to call him. Can I come in?"

Cage was out with a swimsuit model that apparently had a thing for college baseball players. I knew from the way he talked he didn't intend to come up for air much tonight. He'd never answer her call and I hated to see her get more upset than she already was. A horrible thought crossed my mind, surely he hadn't gotten this girl pregnant. Couldn't he see how freaking innocent she was.

"Uh, yeah but I don't know if he'll answer. He's busy... tonight."

She shot me a sour smile and nodded stepping around me.

"I know the kind of busy he is but he'll talk to me."

She sounded rather confident. I wasn't feeling her confidence myself.

"Do you have a cell I can use?"

I reached into the pocket of my jeans and handed it to her unable to argue with her further. She had stopped crying and I wanted to keep it that way.

"Thanks, I'll try calling first."

I watched as she walked over to the sofa and dropped her suitcase to the floor with a thunk before sinking dejectedly down onto the worn cushions as if she'd been here a hundred times. Being as I'd only been moved in for two days, I wouldn't know if she had been here before or not. Cage was a friend of a friend who had been looking for a roommate. I needed somewhere to live fast and his place was nice. Preston was on the same baseball team as Cage at the local community college. Once Preston heard I needed a place to live he called Cage and hooked me up.

"It's me. I left my phone when I ran. You're not here but your new roommate let me in. Call me," she sniffed then hung up. I watched fascinated as she proceeded to text him. She really believed the male whore I lived with was going to call her right up as soon as he got her message. I was intrigued and growing more concerned by the minute.

She finished and handed the phone back to me. A smile touched her red splotchy face and two dimples appeared in her cheeks. Damn that was cute.

"Thanks, do you mind if I wait a little bit until he calls back?"

I shook my head, "No, not at all. You want a drink?" She nodded and stood up.

"Yes, but I'll get it. My drinks are in the bottom drawer of the fridge behind the Bud Lights."

I frowned and followed her into the kitchen. She opened the fridge and bent down to get her hidden drink. With her bent over digging for her so called drink the snug fit of the faded jeans over her ass was hard to miss. It was a perfect heart shape and although she wasn't very tall her legs seemed to go on for miles.

"Ah, here it is. Cage needs to run to the store and restock. He must be letting his one nighters drink my Jarritos."

I couldn't keep guessing. I needed to know who she was exactly. Surely she wasn't one of his girlfriends. Could she be the sister Preston had mentioned dating? I sure as hell hoped not. I was interested and I hadn't been interested in anyone in awhile. Not since the last girl broke my heart. I opened my mouth to ask her how she knew Cage when the phone in my pocket started ringing. She walked over to me and held out her hand. The girl really believed it was Cage. I glanced down and sure enough, my roommate had called back.

She took the phone from my hand.

"Hey"

"She's such a selfish jerk."

"I can't stay there Cage."

"I didn't mean to leave my phone. I was just upset."

"Yes, your new roommate's a nice guy. He's been very helpful."

"No, don't end your date. Get her out of your system. I'll wait."

"I promise not to go back."

"She is who she is Cage."

"I just hate her," I could hear the tears in her voice again.

"No, no, really I'm fine. I just needed to see you."

"Don't. I'll leave."

"Cage --"

"*No*"

"Cage"

"Okay fine."

She held the phone out to me, "He wants to talk to you."

This conversation was like nothing I'd expected. The girl had to be his sister.

"Hey."

"Listen, I need you to make sure Low stays there until I can get home. She's upset and I don't want her leaving. Get her one of her damn Mexican soda thingys out of the fridge. They're behind the Bud

Lights in the bottom drawer. I have to hide them from other chicks I have over. All females tend to like those nasty drinks. Turn on the television, distract her, whatever. I'm only ten minutes away but I'm putting my jeans on as we speak and headed home. Just help get her mind off things but DON'T touch her."

"Ah, okay sure. Is she your sister?"

Cage chuckled into the phone. "Hell no she ain't my sister. I'd never buy my damn sister drinks and call her back when I'm in the middle of a fucking threesome. Low's the girl I'm gonna marry."

I had no response for that. My eyes found her standing over by the window with her back to me. The long thick copper locks curled on the ends and brushed against the middle of her back. She was absolutely nothing like the girls Cage regularly hooked up with. What did he mean she was the girl he was going to marry? That made no sense.

"Keep her there man. I'm on my way."

Then he hung up the phone.

I dropped the phone on the table and stood there staring at her back. She turned around slowly and studied me a moment then a smiled broke across her face.

"He told you he was going to marry me didn't he," she said laughing softly before taking a drink of the orange soda with what appeared to have spanish writing on it.

"Crazy boy. I shouldn't have bothered him but he's all I've got."

She walked over and sank back down onto the old faded green sofa pulling her legs up underneath her.

"Don't worry. I'm not leaving. He'd rip apart my sister's house searching for me and scare the bejesus out of her if I left. I've got enough issues where she's concerned. I don't intend to unleash Cage on her."

I slowly made my way over to the only chair in the room and sat down.

"So, you're engaged?" I asked staring down at her bare ring finger.

With a sad smile she shook her head.

"Not in a million years. Cage has crazy ideas. Just because he says them doesn't make them true."

She raised her eyebrows and took another drink of her soda.

"So, you aren't going to marry Cage," I really would love for her to clarify this because I was incredibly confused and more than a little interested in her. She bit down on her bottom lip and I noticed for the first time how full it was.

"Cage was my 'boy next door' growing up. He's my best friend. I love him dearly and he really is all I have. The only person I can count on. We've never actually been in a relationship before because he knows I won't have sex with him and he needs sex. He's also real wrapped up in the whole idea that a relationship between the two of us before we get married will end badly and he'll lose me. He has this irrational fear of losing me."

Did she know the guy had bagged over three different girls this week and apparently was having a threesome when she'd called? She was so much better than Cage.

"Wipe that look off your face. I don't need your pity. I know what Cage is like. I know you have probably seen the kind of girls he's attracted to and I look absolutely nothing like them. I don't live in a fantasy world. I'm very aware," she tilted her head and smiled at me sweetly, "I don't even know your name."

"Marcus Hardy"

"Well Marcus Hardy, I'm Willow Montgomery but everyone calls me Low. It's a pleasure to meet you."

"Likewise"

"So, you're a friend of Preston's."

I nodded, "Yes but don't hold it against me."

She laughed for the first time and the sudden pleasure from such a simple sound startled me. I liked hearing her laugh.

"I won't. Preston isn't all that bad. He likes to use those pretty boy looks of his to get his way but I'm safe from his attention. Cage would kill him if he decided to bat his baby blues at me."

Was it because of Preston's womanizing or the fact he was a guy that made Cage protective of Willow. Did he really expect her to wait around until he was ready to settle down and marry her?

"LOW," Cage's voice rang out as the door to the apartment swung open. His head snapped around and his eyes went straight to Willow.

"God baby I was so afraid you'd leave, come here." This was a side of Cage I'd never seen. Apparently the sweet little red head got to him in a way no one else could. He pulled her up into his arms, reached down and grabbed the forgotten suitcase then led her back to his bedroom whispering to her the entire way. If she hadn't informed me that she refused to have sex with him earlier I'd have been eat up with righteous fury at the idea of him touching someone so sweet after having just left the bed of not one but two girls. But instead, I was eaten up with envy because I knew he was going to get to hold her and listen to her musical voice as she spilled out all her problems. He'd be the one to fix them, not me. I'd just met her. Why the hell did that bother me?

The Vincent Boys

Chapter 1

Ashton

Why couldn't I have just made it home without seeing them? I wasn't in the mood to play good freaking Samaritan to Beau and his trashy girlfriend. Although he wasn't here, Sawyer would expect me to stop. With a frustrated groan, I slowed down and pulled up beside Beau, who had put some distance between him and his vomiting girlfriend. Apparently throw up wasn't a mating call for him. "Where's your truck parked Beau?" I asked in the most annoyed tone I could muster. He flashed me that stupid sexy grin he knew made every female in town melt at his feet. I'd like to believe I was immune, after all these years, but I wasn't. Being immune to the town's bad boy was impossible.

"Don't tell me perfect little Ashton Gray is gonna offer to help me out," he drawled leaning down to stare at me through my open window.

"Sawyer's out of town so the privilege falls to me. He wouldn't let you drive home drunk and neither will I."

He chuckled sending a shiver of pleasure down my spine. God. He even laughed sexy. "Thanks beautiful but I can handle this. Once Nic stops puking I'll throw her in my truck. I can drive the three miles to her house. You run on along now. Don't you have a bible study somewhere you should be at?"

Arguing with him was pointless. He would just start throwing out more snide comments until he had me so mad I couldn't see straight. I pressed the gas and turned into the parking lot. Like I was going to be able to just leave and let him drive home drunk. He could infuriate me with a wink of his eye and I worked real hard at being nice to everyone. I scanned the parked cars for his old black Chevy truck. Once I spotted it, I walked over to him and held out my hand.

"Either you can give me the keys to your truck or I can go digging for them. What's it going to be Beau? You want me searching your pockets?"

A crooked grin touched his face. "As a matter of fact, I think I might just enjoy you digging around in my pockets Ash. Why don't we go with option number two."

Heat rose up my neck and left splotches of color on my cheeks. I didn't need a mirror to know I was blushing like an idiot. Beau never made suggestive comments to me or even flirted with me. I happened to be the only reasonably attractive female at school he completely ignored.

"Don't you dare touch him, you stupid bitch. His keys are in the ignition of his truck," Nicole, Beau's on again off again girlfriend, lifted her head slinging her dark brown hair back over her shoulder and snarled at me. Bloodshot blue eyes filled with hate watched me as if daring me to touch what was hers. I didn't respond to her nor did I look back up at Beau. Instead, I turned and headed for his truck reminding myself I was doing this for Sawyer.

"Come on then and get in the truck," I barked at both of them before sliding into the driver's seat. It was really hard not to focus on the fact this was the first time I'd ever been in Beau's truck. After countless nights lying on my roof with him talking about the day we got our driver's license and all the places we would go, I was just now, at seventeen years old, sitting inside his truck. Beau picked Nicole up and dumped her in the back.

"Lay down unless you get sick again then make sure you puke over the side," he snapped while opening the driver's side door.

"Hop out princess. She's about to pass out, she won't care if I'm driving."

I gripped the steering wheel tighter.

"I'm not going to let you drive. You're slurring your words. You don't need to drive."

He opened his mouth to argue then mumbled something that sounded like a curse word before slamming the door and walking around the front of the truck to get in on the passenger's side. He didn't say anything and I didn't glance over at him. Without Sawyer around, Beau made me nervous.

"I'm tired of arguing with females tonight. That's the only reason I'm letting you drive," he grumbled without a slur this time. It wasn't surprising he could control the slurring. The boy had been getting drunk before most the kids our age had tasted their first beer. When a guy had a face like Beau's, older girls took notice. He'd been snagging invites to the field parties way before the rest of us.

I managed a shrug. "You wouldn't have to argue with me if you didn't drink so much."

He let out a hard laugh. "You really are a perfect little preacher's daughter aren't you Ash? Once upon a time you were a helluva lot more fun. Before you started sucking face with Sawyer, we use to have some good times together." He was watching me for a reaction. Knowing his eyes were directed at me, made it hard to focus on driving. "You were my partner in crime Ash. Sawyer was the good guy. But the two of us, we were the trouble makers. What happened?"

How do I respond to that? No one knows the girl who use to steal bubble gum from the Quick Stop or abduct the paper boy to tie him up so we could take all his papers and dip them in blue paint before leaving them on the front door steps of houses. No one knew the girl who snuck out of her house at two in the morning to go toilet paper yards and throw water balloons at cars from behind the bushes. No one would even believe I'd done all those things if I told them... no one but Beau.

"I grew up," I finally replied.

"You completely changed Ash."

"We were kids Beau. Yes, you and I got into trouble and Sawyer got us out of trouble but we were just kids. I'm different now."

For a moment he didn't respond. He shifted in his seat and I knew his gaze was no longer focused on me. We'd never had this conversation before. Even if it was uncomfortable, I knew it was way overdue. Sawyer always stood in the way of Beau and I mending our fences. Fences that crumbled and I never knew why. One day he was Beau, my best friend. The next day he was just my boyfriend's cousin.

"I miss that girl, you know. She was exciting. She knew how to have fun. This perfect little preacher's daughter who took her place sucks."

His words hurt. Maybe because they were coming from him or maybe because I understood what he was saying. It wasn't as if I never thought about that girl. I hated him for making me miss her too. I worked really hard at keeping her locked away. Having someone actually want her to be set loose made it so much harder to keep her under control.

"I'd rather be a preacher's daughter than a drunk whore who vomits all over herself." I snapped before I could stop myself. A low chuckle startled me and I glanced over as Beau sunk down low enough in his seat so his head rested on the worn leather instead of the hard window behind him.

"I guess you're not completely perfect. Sawyer'd never call someone a name. Does he know you use the word whore?"

This time I gripped the steering wheel so tightly my knuckles turned white. He was trying to make me mad and he was doing a fabulous job. I had no response to his question. The truth was, Sawyer would be shocked I'd called someone a whore. Especially his cousin's girlfriend.

"Loosen up Ash, it's not like I'm going to tell on you. I've been keeping your secrets for years. I like knowing my Ash is still there somewhere underneath that perfect facade."

I refused to look at him. This conversation was going somewhere I didn't want it to go.

"No one is perfect. I don't pretend to be," which was a lie and we both knew it. Sawyer was perfect and I worked hard to be worthy. The whole town knew I fell short of Sawyer's glowing reputation.

Beau let out a short hard laugh. "Yes Ash, you do pretend to be."

I pulled into Nicole's driveway. Beau didn't move.

"She's passed out. You're going to have to help her," I whispered afraid he'd hear the hurt in my voice.

"You want me to help a vomiting whore?" he asked with an amused tone.

I sighed and finally glanced over at him. He reminded me of a fallen angel with the moonlight casting a glow on his sun kissed blond hair. His eyelids were heavier than usual and his thick eyelashes almost concealed the hazel color underneath.

"She's your girlfriend. Help her." I managed to sound angry. When I let myself study Beau this closely, it was hard to get disgusted with him. I could still see the little boy I'd once thought hung the moon staring back at me. Our past would always be there keeping us from ever really being close again.

"Thanks for reminding me," he said reaching for the door handle without breaking his eye contact with me. I dropped my gaze to study my hands now folded in my lap. Nicole fumbled around in the back of the truck causing it to shake gently reminding us she was back there. After a few more silent moments he finally opened the door.

Beau carried Nicole's limp body to the door and knocked. It opened and he walked inside. I wondered who opened the door. Was it Nicole's mom? Did she care her daughter was passed out drunk? Was she letting Beau take her up to her room? Would Beau stay with her? Crawl in bed with her and fall asleep? Beau reappeared in the doorway before my imagination got too carried away.

Once he was back inside the truck I cranked it up and headed for the trailer park where he lived.

"So tell me Ash, is your insistence to drive home the drunk guy and his whore girlfriend because you're the perpetual good girl who helps everyone? 'Cause I know you don't like me much so I'm curious as to why you want to make sure I get home safe?"

"Beau you're my friend. Of course I like you. We've been friends since we were five. Sure we don't hang out anymore or go terrorizing the neighborhood together but I still care about you."

"Since when?"

"Since when what?"

"Since when do you care about me?"

"That is a stupid question Beau. You know I've always cared about you," I replied. Even though I knew he wouldn't let such a vague answer fly. The truth was I never really talked to him much anymore. Nicole was normally wrapped around one of his body parts. And when he spoke to me it was always to make some wise crack.

"You hardly acknowledge my existence," he replied.

"That's not true."

He chuckled. "We sat by each other in history all year and you hardly ever glanced my way. At lunch you never look at me and I sit at the same table you do. We're at the field parties every weekend and if you ever turn your superior gaze in my direction it's normally with a disgusted expression. So, I'm a little shocked you still consider me a friend."

The large live oak trees signaled the turn into the trailer park Beau had lived all is life. The rich beauty of the southern landscape as you pulled onto the gravel road was deceiving. Once I drove passed the large trees, the scenery drastically changed. Weathered trailers with old cars up on blocks and battered toys scattered the yards. More than one window was covered by wood or plastic. I didn't gawk at my surroundings. Even the man sitting on his porch steps in nothing but his underwear and a cigarette hanging out of his mouth didn't surprise me. I knew this trailer park well. It was a part of my childhood. I came to a stop in front of Beau's trailer. It would be easier to believe this was the alcohol talking but I knew it wasn't. We hadn't been alone in over four years. Since the moment I became Sawyer's girlfriend, our relationship had changed.

I took a deep breath then turned to look at Beau. "I never talk in class. Not to anyone but the teacher. You never talk to me at lunch so I have no reason to look your way. Attracting your attention leads to you making fun of me. And, at the field, I'm not looking at you with disgust. I'm looking at Nicole with disgust. You could really do much better than her." I stopped myself before I said anything stupid.

He tilted his head to the side as if studying me. "You don't like Nicole much do you. You don't have to worry about her hang up with Sawyer. He knows what he's got and he isn't going to mess it up. Nicole can't compete with you."

Nicole had a thing for Sawyer? She was normally mauling Beau. I'd never picked up on her liking Sawyer. I knew they'd been an item in seventh grade for like a couple of weeks but that was junior high school. It didn't really count. Besides she was with Beau. Why would she be interested in anyone else?

"I didn't know she liked Sawyer," I replied still not sure I believed him. Sawyer was so not her type.

"You sound surprised," Beau replied.

"Well I am actually. I mean, she has you. Why does she want Sawyer?"

A pleased smile touched his lips making his hazel eyes light up. I realized I hadn't exactly meant to say something he could misconstrue the way he was obviously doing.

He reached for the door handle before pausing and glancing back at me.

"I didn't know my teasing bothered you Ash. I'll stop."

That hadn't been what I was expecting him to say. Unable to think of a response I sat there holding his gaze.

"I'll get your car switched back before your parents see my truck at your house in the morning." He stepped out of the truck and I watched him walk toward the door of his trailer with one of the sexiest swaggers known to man. Beau and I had needed to have this talk. Even if my imagination was going to go wild for a while, where he was concerned. My secret attraction to the town's bad boy had to remain a secret.

The next morning I found my car parked in the drive way as promised with a note wedged under the windshield wipers. I reached for it and a small smile touched my lips.

"Thanks for last night. I've missed you," he had simply signed it "B"

Coming Soon:

The Vincent Brothers 6/5/12

(The Vincent Boys #2)

WHILE IT LASTS 8/7/12

(Sea Breeze Series #3)

CEASELESS 9/18/12

(Existence #3)

Acknowledgments

I have to start by thanking Keith, my husband, who tolerated the dirty house, lack of clean clothes, and my mood swings, while I wrote this book (and all my other books).

My three precious kiddos who ate a lot of corn dogs, pizza, and Frosted Flakes because I was locked away writing. I promise, I cooked them many good hot meals once I finished.

Tammara Webber, my critique partner. When Tammara suggested we become critique partners I had a major "fan girl" moment. I adore her Between the Lines series. And of course I immediately JUMPED on that offer. Tammara's advice, edits, and friendship are all major factors in the creation of Predestined. She's brilliant and I'm honored to be able to call her my CP as well as friend.

Monica Tucker, my best friend and Becky Potts, my mother: these two are in competition for title of my biggest fan. They both read Predestined and helped catch typos, point out problems in the story and faithfully cheered me on.

My FP girls. I'm choosing not to share what FP stands for because my mother may read this and it will give her heart failure. Kidding... maybe. You girls make me laugh, listen to me vent, and always manage to give me some eye candy to make my day brighter. You are truly my posse.

Stephanie Mooney who is the best cover artist ever. She is brilliant and I shout it to the roof tops on a regular basis.

Stephanie T. Lott for her incredible job at editing Predestined. I can not express how thankful I am to have found her. *Points back up to where I mentioned Tammara Webber and her genius*
I have her to thank for directing me to Stephanie.

The Paranormal Plumes http:// www.theplumessociety.com/ are a group of YA paranormal writers that I absolutely adore. We travel together to hold book signings and we support each other in our writing ups and downs. I love each and every one of them.

About the Author

Abbi Glines can be found hanging out with rockstars, taking out her yacht on weekends for a party cruise, sky diving, or surfing in Maui. Okay maybe she needs to keep her imagination focused on her writing only. In the real world, Abbi can be found hauling kids (several who seem to show up that don't belong to her) to all their social events, hiding under the covers with her MacBook in hopes her husband won't catch her watching Buffy on Netflix again, and sneaking off to Barnes and Noble to spend hours lost in the yummy goodness of books. If you want to find her then check Twitter first because she has a severe addiction to tweeting @abbiglines. She also blogs regularly but rarely about anything life changing. She also really enjoys talking about herself in third person. www.abbiglines.com